The Memoirs of an
EMPRESS

D1566263

ZYLIA N. KNOWLIN

NEWMAN SPRINGS PUBLISHING
320 Broad Street
Red Bank, NJ 07701

First originally published by Newman Springs Publishing 2019

ISBN 978-1-64096-889-9 (Paperback)
ISBN 978-1-64096-890-5 (Digital)

Printed in the United States of America

CONTENTS

INTRODUCTION

Life is a journey of daily experiences that when summed up will tell the story of your life. Be a leader of your own destiny, take life by the hand, and dance with it. Time is the only thing in life you cannot exchange, delete, or increase, so make the best of it.

I have learned that in times of hurt, you must heal yourself and never depend on others to comfort you. Find peace in our King and know that you are royalty, so show others the same.

My life has been and continues to be a road with many detours, but I have learned to think big, aim high, and work for what you want.

Be inspired, be loved, be noticed, but most of all, be true to yourself.

"To thine self, be true."

Thank you for your continued love and for the support with this publication.

Zylia N. Knowlin

EATING SOUSE

Walking into the kitchen, I could smell a very interesting smell. It damn near knocked me off my feet. I walked into the kitchen and could hear the laughter and cheers of those within. I moved closer intrigued at this point to know what it is I'm smelling.

"What is that? it looks different." I said to my man, standing next to me. I was so proud to be his wife, and everywhere we went, I always kept a steady smile to remind everyone of that fact. It was about 8:00 pm, and we had just arrived at his mother's house. She lived there with her son and his wife Lynda who had recently had a baby herself. It was a small apartment cramped with many people that were there to participate in the festivities. "It's Souse, a Nali dish that is served pickled, it's often made from pork, so I know you wouldn't eat it..." said Gary, my husband of three years. *Damn Skippy*, I'm thinking to myself. *I will never in my life eat anybody's swine. And it's pickled, hell no*, I continue thinking. *I cannot believe they're here eating this stuff.* I continue walking into the living room to sit on the couch hoping to avoid that dreaded smell.

To my surprise, I saw everyone going in, munching chewing, drinking; no one seems the least bothered by my lack of comfort. While there were so many dishes available, not being from Nali, I'm scared to taste anything not sure what it might be made from. I heard the voice of the one who brought me here, my love. I'm thinking to myself, *doesn't he see that I just don't fit in here and that I am uncomfortable?* He came to sit next to me, so closely. While he continued conversing with his family and friends, I sat there pretending that we were all one big family, but it all felt so fake. He leaned over to kiss me; I could smell the souse on his breathe; it was starting to make me sick!

I began to get up, and head toward the bathroom having to once again pass the pot of souse. I froze and looked at it carefully now; it's like jelly; it smelled like vinegar, and it had so much onions in it. Now I was determined to get into the bathroom as fast as I can. I locked the door. I was surrounded by pink plastic curtains and pink rugs. And the smell of roach spray added to the nausea that I was feeling. I wished I could just throw up and pretend that I was too sick to stay for the party.

Alas, I pulled myself together, washed off my face, and decided to try this family bonding thing again. I flushed the toilet, so everyone thought I really had to use it; this was a trick I often used when I needed a few minutes alone where no other place was available. Walking through the bedroom this time, I avoided the pot. I quickly sat back down on the couch next to my love and continued to listen to their stories of back home.

As soon as I could say "boo," his mother jumped into the conversation saying: "So, you see Stephanie will be coming over on Friday night, you must pick her up by 7:00 pm." I just wanted to stab her; it seemed to me that she's always meddling into affairs especially of those that she had no business.

All the while, I was sitting here thinking, *is this man going to tell him mom to butt out of our affairs?* "Stephanie has to see her therapist on Monday so make sure you get her a nice outfit for the appointment. I believe her mother also told me she needs some juice, milk, and cheese too."

"Ok," he replied and then turned to me. I was sitting here thinking *why this man was looking at me? I had nothing to do with this mess your mom was encouraging.*

It was just last month that Gary and Keyshana (Gary's baby mother) had gotten into a fight at his mom's house because his mom had invited her there for Thanksgiving dinner knowing that his wife would be there as well. To this day, I will never figure out why she would invite the baby momma to Thanksgiving dinner knowing that Gary and she did not get along.

She obviously could not give two s—— that I was going to be there. It was some argument, so I heard; to tell you the truth, I could not really tell you what was actually said since I got up and walked out of the house with my five-month-old baby while the whole thing was going down. *F——this*, I thought, *this woman is so low class*, me referring to his mother. It's no wonder why she was never married. Looking back at that relationship, that's why I never had any respect for his mother because she was rude, disrespectful, and pretentious with me.

While they were arguing, I took myself up, got my car keys, and drove my baby and me right on home, that was my first Thanksgiving with his family. That was one of those memories that never fade.

I was finally able to get Gary's attention after he seemed to be in such great thought, trying to give the signal that I was ready to leave. I asked him if he was finished eating his souse because I was hoping that would signal him to start making his exit; furthermore, I just couldn't take the smell that came from his bowl anymore. "Yes," he replied. "Oh good, let me take that bowl for you." I got up and put the bowl in the sink. While in the kitchen, I noticed that there was a picture of Stephanie and her mother on the refrigerator.

The picture itself did not bother me, but what made me upset was the fact that the Christmas picture I mailed to this house with my baby, and her parents hadn't made unto that same place.

A great sadness came over me at that instance. I sank a little inside, and at that moment I knew that these people would never be my family. I loved to take family pictures for the holidays and proudly mailed them out to everyone whose address I had. To imagine that my firstborn's grandmother did not see it prudent to include her granddaughter's picture on the refrigerator as she did for the other grandchildren's pictures that were displayed.

I had a choice to make at that time but never knew it. The choice was mine, but I did not make it. Did I want to live my life forever in this manner? Was I content with playing second-line to his family, or did I want or need to be loved by my in-laws? Did I want to continue building my family not worrying about his family, or did I want my baby to grow up without her father? Did I want to disappoint my family, or did I want to prove to the world that I could succeed in this marriage? I was so determined to see this work. After all, there was nothing at this point that I could not make work.

"I'm just going to hold on the promise of this marriage," I said to myself. "For better or for worse, in richness and poverty, till death do I part?" That was the vow.

After yet another long hour of loud talking and places in Nali I knew nothing about, we finally made it home. "Hey honey, I'm going to take the baby in her room and get her ready for bed," I told Gary. I was so glad to be home. I gathered all the necessary items in the crib leaving my baby in her floor seat, while I walked toward the bathroom to prepare the water for her bath. She was sitting in her little seat on the floor which she just loved playing with the toys that are attached to the front bar. She giggled and cooed; she looked at me with all hopes and dreams. She was to be my future, my all, and if I was to give her the best, I had to give her the opportunity to know and love her father. I loved him so much after all, and I wanted us to have the perfect family or at least what I thought the perfect family was.

"I'm coming baby—" I gently reminded her that I was just in the bathroom.

Finally, the water is caught, perfect for my baby, not too cold, not too hot, warm. I turned around to gather her towel and noticed my face in the mirror. There's a tear. I quickly wiped it off, but as I wiped, more fell. And fell. And fell. I'm crying. Being so frustrated about the events of the evening, I was becoming emotional quickly. The fact that I will have to deal with this lady just made me ill. All I could think was that she will never accept me or my daughter.

It had disgusted me to think that I helped him file for citizenship for her because I thought she was going to be my mother-in-law, turned out she hated me. Before she even stepped foot in this country, I told Gary that I could not wait to meet her, I had wanted to thank her for giving birth to my husband. I was never able to tell her that because I never, ever felt comfortable talking to her.

I believed with all my heart that she wished that Gary would have married Keyshana instead of me. Keyshana and her mother were Gary's mom's friend from Nali. Marcia (his mother) told me they were friends. I guess this was her justification as to why she "had" to be friends with Keyshana. I believed it to be the reason why I would never be accepted by her, at least not for her son.

Years later, Marcia told me during some random conversation that we were having, that I was never a real woman because I never had any sons. I wonder if she knew that she was never a real woman because she wasn't a lady.

The baby began to cry, and I realized that it has taken me almost three minutes to gather my composure, not once did Gary get up to see why the baby was crying. I wish I could see with my eyes. I wish my eyes were open instead of closed.

"I'm coming my sweets," I wiped my eyes with my towel and grabbed my baby so tight. I held her so close whispering, "You are my future, you are my life, and I will always be there for you my baby, always." I rocked her forgetting that the water was now beginning to get cold.

What is wrong with me? I was here sitting here thinking to myself. I continued to tend to the baby all the while he sat in the couch, resting. "I'm putting some souse in the microwave, do you want some?" He yelled into the room. He could not be possibly talking to me, could he? Did he not notice anything that took place tonight? "No, thank you" I responded. He's watching the basketball game, I proceeded to putting the baby and her chair into the bedroom so that I could write in my journal:

Dear Diary:

I hope I know what I'm doing. I went to dinner with Gary tonight at his mom's house, and it was a nightmare. I love going out, but I hate when I finally do, I'm worrying, instead of enjoying my time away from my responsibilities. I wish I can convince Marcia to give me a chance, but it seems like she just doesn't get it. I had always had hopes that I would have a mother-in-law like my mom had, an awesome one. How could I compare her to my mom? After all, she spent a whole lifetime hating her own sister; who does that? Look how closely my mom is with her sister and I with my sisters, even the one I'm not close to. I don't hate her; I love her in my own unique way.

Anyway, Stephanie will be here tomorrow. God help me. I know she's a little special, but I just cannot take when she's around. Gary acts so different with her. He buys her things, even when the kids are together he will buy her something but not Destiney. He tells me that Destiney does not need whatever it is, but he does not understand how children think. Children naturally get jealous when one gets something and the other does not. I hope things get better around here. I really love my family, but do they love me?

Empress

⚜

By the time I finished writing in my journal, the baby had rocked herself to sleep, which made me happy because I was ready for a quiet moment. I got up to put her in the crib when I realized that Gary was in the living room fixing himself a drink; let me see if he offers me one. I guess he forgot to ask me because he never did. Heading in the bathroom to take my own shower, I turned on the facet. As soon as I turned on the shower, here goes the tears again. This time they seemed like they never stop. Tear one; tear two; tear me down; that's the truth. They often say that tears heal the soul; you know, I believed that. After a good cry, I always seemed to feel much better.

I finally came out the shower and went into the kitchen. The sink had a few dishes in it still. That's like one of my pet peeves. I hated a sink full of dishes. The same stinky souse bowl was sitting there. God. But why were these dishes in the sink when I just bathed the baby, put her to sleep, and tidied up the bathroom? I have no answer. Still I proceed to the sink to empty it of its contents. Perhaps I was also emptying myself of my self-pride. I gazed through the window and remembered a time. I was ten years old, and I could hear my father's voice. "Get down stairs and help me fry this chicken."

I always thought my dad made the best fried chicken.

At that same moment, I remembered that the dishes were still sitting there waiting for me, all clean now and so am I. Fresh.

After looking out the window once again, I turned toward the living room and went to sit down on the couch. Now this was the life I thought to myself. It must be nice to just come home and plop yourself down for hours not having a care in the world. He's watching the basketball game, so I'm just pretending like I'm watching it too. If I didn't sit here and watch this TV, I'm definitely going to fall asleep. *I rather watched the TV out here*, I thought *because I did not want to wake the baby up, by turning on the TV in the bedroom.* The only time I "liked" watching basketball was when they paid me in college to keep stats. And those were some good times as well.

This game was making me so bored, I thought to myself. Not knowing what to do with myself, I started arranging the picture frames on the bar stand. *They looked perfect now,* I was thinking, so I sat back on my perfect couch, in my perfect living room, with my perfect husband in my perfect world. PERFECT.

"I have never seen such a perfect couple," said Wanda and Jefferson as they entered the party. "This is the best Christmas party the company has given in a few years," said Wanda. "It really is a lovely affair," I replied. The girls were having such a lovely time. I could feel the excitement of the holidays in the air. The children were running around; there were decorations, prizes, face painting, story time; you can even take a picture with Santa; we didn't know where to begin. "The girls have gotten so big and how they are so beautiful," Enid commented. I always loved being around Gary's coworkers because they were so intrigued by us. They always made me feel so proud to be his wife. After all, we were a young couple, had two beautiful girls, owned our cars, had careers, and we were young with so much promise ahead. They also appreciated the fact that I sent them Christmas cards for the holidays and was always such a pleasure to be around and talk to on the phone; they had often commented. Calvin was one of my favorites; he was always such a prankster, and he liked to remind Gary of what sometimes happened at college since Gary never went. Gary not going to college meant he did not understand some of the jokes Calvin would tell me. We would joke about frat parties and silly things we did going away to school and being away from home.

"Destiney and Vanessa come back here," I yelled while they ignored me, running off after the life-size Pikachu character that was playing with the children. "There you go," I said to my sister. I finally found Jazmine wandering around. After I arrived at the party, she was now free to enjoy the festivities. She brought the children to the party for me since I had to work late that day. We both knew coming late to the party might mean that the kids having to miss out on some of the festivities, so she volunteered to take them. In any case, she loved getting out the house. The way I felt was Jazmine's the best sister in the world; she will do anything for her family, and I was glad to be a part of that. Meanwhile, it was face-painting time.

The kids were done, and Jazmine got her tattoo done and so did I. We stuffed a few snacks in the stroller and headed toward the picture station. It was so thoughtful that the company would have this here because so many of their employees never got time to spend with their children because they are busy working so hard. It was kind of that way with Gary; he did spend a lot of hours at work, so I often excused him from many of the responsibilities of being a father.

So many of my girlfriends would brag how their husbands would do dishes and laundry and other chores. I never ever heard any of the wives say they took out garbage. I was the only one. I often excused his inability or lack of attention to these matters because he worked long hours, sometimes having to go in the office on the weekends. I was never doubtful that indeed he was working and trying to do what he could for his family. So I excused him from many responsibilities I knew a man was supposed to have when he has a family of his own. I soon learned that excuses are the mountains that we build kingdoms of nothingness.

My best friend would always joke about her husband as him being the only one in house that could touch the washing machine. I was always jealous of her marriage because it seemed to be so perfect. I later learned that she had some skeletons in her closet and that a smile is often a mask as it was in my case. I often laughed with her and told her it was because she did not know how to use technology that was why she couldn't operate the washing machine.

Deep down, I wished my husband would be like that too.

She would tell me about her husband cutting out coupons and looking for sales on laundry soap because that was his job. Another friend yelled at me when I told her I would sometimes iron for four hours on the weekend on top of cooking. I never once told Lisa the other chores I did on the weekend; she would kill me! Lisa would say just stop doing things and see what happens. She especially hated the fact that I spread the beds and washed dishes before I would leave the house in the morning before going to work. Some of my neighbors would even see me scraping the snow off my car and say, "Sis, you need help—" I would just brush it off. "Nah, I'm good Son." This was how it would be for fourteen years.

Dear Diary:

Today I took the kids over to my mom's house, so I can get a break. I feel so bad that whenever I want to go out, I always have to rely on her but the truth of the matter, it's like to their other grandmother, they don't exist. She didn't even buy them gifts this year for Christmas. Gary says it's because she doesn't have money like my mom. I kept telling him those were just excuses.

I told him that Christmas comes the same time every year, and she should buy gifts throughout the year like I do so that when the holidays come by, she's covered. I went to Save More and bought them a lot of little toys for under $10 just today. He always makes excuses for her. Sometimes I can't even open my closet with the number of gifts I have stashed in the closet. It's okay because they are still going to have an awesome Christmas.

Stephanie is here tonight. I finally bought a futon the other day, so she has somewhere to sleep besides the floor. I definitely did not want her sleeping in the same bed with the kids; she always seems to have a cold. Gary went and bought her toys and clothes for Christmas. He did not even buy a pair of socks for our kids. He said he's going to buy them whatever they did not get; we'll see. I heard that before. He also went by his mom's and picked up some pepper pot she made and bread. We always have that on Christmas morning; it's one of my favorite Nali dishes. I know that he bought me a necklace because he kept asking me what kind of necklace I liked when we went to the store the other day. He does buy a lot of gold; perhaps he sees me as his trophy wife! He often tells me that he knew he would marry an Indian girl. Don't get me wrong, my friend. I love him very much. I just wish he could see things my way sometimes. Merry Christmas.

Empress

✦

This was going to be the best party, ever and I have given some parties over the years. I kept thinking as I prepared the house for the bash that was to come that night. I definitely should have seen this coming, in retrospect. I sat here thinking. My dang-on third eye was on that day.

I was so excited about this party but sad at the same time. I am having a fortieth party for Gary today, and it's been so hectic. I've been running around like a nut for the last three weeks, placing orders, making phone calls, pricing items needed for the party, etc. I just want everything to be flawless. It's going to be a black-and-white party. Aubrey is playing, and he's bringing his light effects like he had for our wedding.

I have transformed my second floor into a dance hall. The balloons glistened in the lights; the cakes were gorgeous; the favors were already set with the straight pins in them; the liquor has been chilled; and the food choices were endless. I didn't even want to get into how much I spent on liquor. *I know he's going to be so surprised*, is what I'm thinking right now. Currently his best friend Michael had him on the road until about midnight that gives me about three hours left before guests started to arrive.

I began to head on upstairs because the place looked seamless, so at this point, it was time for me to go get ready. "We're on the way," I just received the call. Lord, I'm not ready. That was the signal that soon Gary would be at the door ready for his party. Still putting the finishing touches on my accessories and makeup. I knew I had to hurry up.

Done.

I rushed downstairs and told Aubrey, aka Mr. DJ, to turn off the lights because the man of the hour was on the way. I instructed the guests to be quiet and began telling them that when Gary arrives, we shout out "Happy Birthday." They agreed, continued talking but bringing their voices to a low hush. I peeked out the window to see his truck being double-parked. The two men got out of the vehicle laughing and reminiscing about the old times. Soon I heard the keys jingle. All is quiet on the other side of the door. Until the key turns and slowly left the keyhole.

"Surprise, Happy Birthday!" we all screamed out loud. His face was a sheer delight. The music resumed. His face was of disbelief. He smiled so bright we could feel his sincere disbelief and wonder. He must have been thinking, *how did she do this*, I often wondered.

I was so angry with him the days before this party; I was sure he wasn't expecting dinner out much less a party of this magnitude. He had been frustrating me with his whole attitude. The girls now, 12, 9, and 5, were so much work and a lot of responsibility, and all of this was just tiring me out. I was frustrated. I was over it! I was exhausted with the mere thought of household responsibilities. Despite that fact, I had proposed to myself that perhaps before I give up, I try my best to work on my marriage.

"Here's to you, Gary. Happy Birthday; may Jah show his blessings to you forever more." I lifted my glass and offered up a cheer to my husband. With that, walked in his mother, his sister, and their guests. She was always late and always frowning. In her hand, she carried a dish. I went over to her to see if I could assist her with the dish to the food table.

Suddenly my nose caught a familiar whiff. In the bowl, I could smell vinegar; its contents were light in color, turning my stomach with every breath I took, and I was clearly standing too close to it. It was souse. I wanted to fling it down the block.

Although being married to Gary, he no longer ate pork; so his mother now made the souse with cow's feet. But I did not care, and I wanted it out of my house. *And who asked her to bring this souse to our party*, was all I was thinking. I hated souse and everything it represented to me. The truth was souse never did anything to me. I just never was honest about how it made me feel.

I had to learn that if you don't stand for something, you will fall for anything.

The smell reached in my soul. I couldn't take it anymore; so I uncovered a portion of it, just so that I could look at it. It taunted me, laughed at me; it made me feel out of control in my own home. It still looked slimy, evil. What was wrong with me? I was being jeered by food. I decided to get myself together and went to the kitchen to get a serving spoon for it. I wanted to throw ketchup in it and ruin it. I wanted to ruin it because I blamed his mom for ruining my wonderful hopes of having a pleasant mother-in-law.

I wanted to ruin it before it ruined the party, but it was too late. I had already accepted souse into my life, in my party, and into my home.

I lived with souse for so many years keeping my true feelings hidden. I had allowed souse the power over me; it controlled me. Every time I smelled it, saw it, and thought of it, it weakened my spirit. Why did I not see that I should not sit down at the table with it? Especially in my own home? Why did I not respect myself to maintain my standards? Being that this was my home, I should have maintained dominion over it. But I invited it into my home and then got mad when it actually showed up.

My grandfather would say, "It's not everybody that can eat at my table." I clearly was mistaken when I thought I could break bread with everyone. I always believed that everyone should be given an opportunity to prove themselves. I soon realized that I didn't have to give anyone a chance to disappoint me. If you know that people are trying to tear you down, don't let them. They only have power over you if you give them power in your life. The only way to give them power in your life is to invite them into your life. They can't get in if you don't let them in. I was always very observant except when it came to my own self. Can someone tell me how you can be so smart but so stupid at the same time?

Dear Diary:

Today was a great day. We just came back from Sesame Place. I had a ball and so did the family. It was so hot today. The kids were so happy, and I just loved that place; I cannot wait till we can go back. The drive wasn't so bad either; the children were really good in the car. Gary said he really had a wonderful time. I hoped the next family trip he plans it because I'm getting tired of always planning and paying for these excursions.

I lost one of my favorite bracelets that Gary brought me, must have been while climbing on the ropes with Chrissy. I did not even realize that it was missing until we stopped at the rest stop, and I went to wash my hands. I was so upset. I knew whoever finds it will love it. I knew I loved it; it matched my tri-gold wedding ring. Gary said he would buy me another one; I believed he will.

We took a lot of pictures and brought back a lot of souvenirs. I even found a picture frame with Destiney's name there too. Anyway, I'm pooped, will write back to you another day.

Empress

◦◦◦

Well summer vacation was awesome this year, I thought to myself having to come to grips that I was soon going back in the classroom. Although I worked summer school, I still made the best of it and even took the kids to Virginia this year. I took them to Kings Dominion, and Jazmine came as well. This trip was something that I have been trying to plan for some time now, but Gary could not seem to get the time off from work. Finally, I decided that on the last Friday after summer school grades were entered, I was going to make the trip with my kids, my sister, and myself. I was getting so tired of having to put on hold the things that I wanted to do.

Since I worked summer school, I had the extra money since I needed to pay for everything myself. Gary was so upset that I was going to take this trip without him. He just couldn't understand why in the world I would want to take this trip with my sister. He did not understand that it was not what I really wanted, but it was what I was willing to do to ensure that the children were going to have an adventure this summer.

"So, you're actually going to Virginia without me?" Gary said.

20

"Ummm, yes Gary, I've been asking you all summer if there was going to be time off from your schedule so that we can plan a vacation, and you never got back to me." I said.

"I told you that I just cannot take vacations like that. I have to have notice. My job isn't a union job like yours." he says.

"Gary, my vacations are always the same. I'm a teacher I asked you a while ago to plan to go with us, now come on," I continued to argue.

"And you are taking Jazmine." he stated. "Yes Gary, would you rather me to make the seven- hour trip by myself and the children?" I said quite gingerly. "No, I would rather you not go" he replied.

The conversation—well argument—continued for the next twenty minutes. He never realized that nothing that he would say would not change my mind. I was determined to get out of the city, take my kids with me, and enjoy the time that God had given me. There was going to be no way that I was going to return to work without having taken at least one trip somewhere.

"Do you know that Dahlia is a baby?" He once again started up the conversation, "Well, duh Gary. I had her remember," I snapped back at him. "Listen, I understand that you do not want me traveling with the kids by myself, but I am going and that's final." I once again tried to make my statement heard even more loudly now. In an instance, he was so upset with me; he got his keys and proceeded out the door, slamming it as he walked out.

As soon as he slammed the door, all hopes of getting him to see it my way was out the door.

It made me so heated to know that he would rather walk out on our conversation rather than to finish it. He had always been that way, not really willing to hear sides of an argument if the side wasn't his own. I saw that side of him, yet I never "saw" it.

I just turned back around and walked back in the kitchen, trying hard to not let this argument get the best of me. The children, who were upstairs, were now making their way downstairs. "Do you guys want some macaroni and cheese?" I said to the girls, each one answering, "yes." It's their favorite and not one time did I offer to make it for them did they ever say no. "Okay, ladies. I'll be in the kitchen if you need me." I said to them.

Turning around to head toward the kitchen I could feel my emotions begin to unwind. I reached for the box of macaroni and cheese from the cabinet when I noticed a bottle. It was a medicine bottle with Gary's name on it, but the name of the prescription was scratched off. I never saw this bottle, so it perplexed me as to how it had made it way all the way behind the box I was reaching for. I opened the bottle only to get a whiff on the powdery smell of medicine. I look at it. *This is strange. I've never seen these pills in my house before.* I thought to myself. I closed the bottle back and put it back where I found it, never to make mention to it to Gary.

Taking down the box, I opened it and started to put the macaroni in the water that had already started to boil at this point. My mind was running wild. I emptied the box of the macaroni into the pot and began to stir. Stirring up my feelings of suspense, mystery, and trust, I waited till the macaroni was soften before I poured its content into my strainer. *What could these pills be for?* I began to wonder to myself. Not knowing the answer, I added the cheese to the macaroni in the pot.

"Destiney, you and your sisters go wash your hands and come downstairs for lunch." I yelled upstairs, careful not to scare Dahlia who was sitting in the high chair watching TV.

"Yes, mommy," she answered and told her sisters the same.

I could hear the water running upstairs, so I knew it would not be long before they would be downstairs. So, I tried to gather my composure as quickly as possible.

"Mommy, what's wrong?" Vanessa asked me.

I tried so hard to cover the frustration on my face but she read me like a book.

"Nothing, Honey. I just have some things on my mind, and I'll be fine." I said to her. She stared at me for a minute and went into the dining room.

"Christiana, come on downstairs," I yelled once more upstairs. Destiney made her way into the kitchen and started to get the silverware and cups.

"Mom, what's wrong?" she said to me. "Nothing, Sweetie, I'm okay." I said.

"Mom, is Dad mad because we are going to Virginia without him?" she asked.

"Yes, Destiney, he does not want us to go without him, and he is not going to be able to go before school starts. Do you think we should stay home?" I sought the counsel of my firstborn who was herself only a child. "Mom, I think dad will understand if we go eventually, and we really want to go to Kings Dominion and see aunt May." She said.

"Destiney, you make a lot of sense for a little girl. I love you and thank you." I replied. We continued talking for about five minutes. It was at that time that I realized my children were going to be my rock. It will be them who kept me grounded. To this day, they still are the ones.

Having now returned after being out for five hours, Gary made his way back home. At this point, neither one has much to say. We continued watching TV, ignoring what words we had uttered to one another just a few hours ago. It was hard to believe that any concessions among us were going to be made in this fashion. I was thinking that we might not ever get over this. It was from this point that I noticed Gary's behavior toward my sister and mother became somewhat wayward and distant.

Apparently, he blamed my sister Jazmine and mother for our problems. He often said that I allowed Jazmine the opportunity to advise me on marital affairs that were of no concern to her. He often said that she was disrespectful to him, and I allowed her to be that way. He hated my sister when in fact, she never hated him. I will tell you that in no certain terms will my sister ever allow a man to come between us and neither will she allow her sister to be taken for granted or abused. For many years, my sister served as my confidant which she still does.

I must tell you; where others have failed me, she had always done the best that a little sister could do. Unfortunately, because Gary never had that type of relationship with his siblings, it was a bond that he could not fathom.

There's a lot to be said about laying down with a person who you love. One thing is for sure; you should not lay with a person while you are angry. It makes waking up quite awkward. I also often must remind myself to never forget to love, to lie down by yourself.

⚬⊙⚬

Dear Diary:

What a wonderful time we are having at Kings Dominion; it is hot as hell down here. We are staying at the Howard Linden Hotel which is about two minutes from the park. We spent the entire day at the park today, and I am exhausted. We went to dinner at Silver Diamond, which is one of my favorite buffets. The kids ate so much. After that, we came back to the hotel and went to the pool. Now the kids are asleep. Thank God.

In the morning, we will be going back to the park and doing it all over again except this time, we will be going to Pizza Hut for dinner. We could not get the hut in NYT, so kids will definitely enjoy that. On Sunday, we will be going to spend the day at aunt Lavern's house, and she said that she is going to BBQ. I always loved her steaks, and her house is very lovely too. We will stay with her until Monday and then make our way back to Gullie, sometime Monday evening.

No more summer school, so I'm not rushing to get back. It's been a great mini-vacation so far; so glad I came. I talked to Gary earlier, and he sounded still upset, oh well. Now Jazmine's here, making me a drink. So, we will probably be up for a while talking and bullsh—— so I guess I will talk to you later. If we head back to the pool tonight, don't be surprised; Jazmine loves the pool.

Anyway, Gary said he just came from his mother's house, where he had dinner. He always goes over there for food especially when I'm not around or when he wants his Nali dishes. One thing is for certain, she will cook him anything he wants, anytime, even souse. I'm not even going to go there right now!

I'm about to be out now but soon chat ya!—Adult time.

Oh P.S. While we were in Silver Diamond today, I saw a sign with this motto. I want to write it down so I would never forget it: "When you write the story of your life, make sure you are the one holding the pen." In my case though, I sure hope I'm holding a calligraphy pen!

Empress

THE WEDDING DAY

Nona had just called me and told me that she was coming over to hang out with me a little bit since she was traveling to Mahlia the next day. I had become quite good friends with her although she was much younger than me. There was something about her ambition and determination that attracted me to her personality. We had met up in Mahlia the summer before where we got to know each other on another level. She had even volunteered to bring some items to my family tomorrow when she was going. She said she was going to bring me some Crotyian patties since I loved them so much, and she knew where to get the authentic ones in Florida since she was Crotyian.

While waiting for her to arrive, I decided to label the clothes and shoes I brought for Zoe and Cane so it would be easier for Nona to separate my things from the other things she may be carrying with her to Mahlia. As soon as I had finished labeling the last pair of shoes, she was ringing the doorbell. As she entered, I could smell the flakey, patties filled with codfish; it smelled so good I could hardly wait until she gave me the box. I opened the box and proceeded to eat two patties back-to-back. She had traveled to France the week after work let out and had brought me back an apron that I had proudly displayed in my kitchen. I showed her the apron, and she continued to reminisce about her adventures in Europe. As I listened to her stories, I often wished that I could have been a young, free, and single—woman that could save her money, travel the world, and live vicariously.

Despite how I felt about her, she often reminded me, that she admired my strength as a single parent of African descent and a woman that was working toward achieving all the goals that I have in life. I was chattering about my wishes to travel with her to Mahlia and how sad I was that I was not going to be able to make the trip this summer. As we continued talking, she reminded me that she wanted to see my wedding album. I was always very proud of my wedding day. I had put so much of myself in the planning and preparation of all the events of that day. And even though things did not seem to go the way I had always seen in my marriage, I was still very proud of having the opportunity of wearing a wedding dress. I had seen the looks of some of the unmarried or never married women in my age group, and they were often quite sad from the lack of that experience.

I ran to the closet and pulled out my wedding album. It was a little dusty, but it was still the book of memories that was often locked away in my heart that I never really wanted to show, in or out of the book. It had been nineteen years ago since the wedding day, but the album pictures were still intact, still looked fresh, and still needed to be seen. It was a lovely green leather-covered album engraved with "Mr. and Mrs. Braxton, August 20th, 1997." Its pictures were each bordered with a special album sheet that was lined with gold trimming. The album still looked as beautiful as the day I received it in the mail. Gary and I had used the same company No Whaoosss to photograph our wedding, to create the videos, and to create the thank-you notes that were sent out to the guests after the wedding day. At the time, I was so concerned about making sure I had the best that money could buy, and after all these years, I could see in the quality of the photos and video that I had made a wise decision.

Nona had just returned to the living room after using the restroom, and I had already had the wedding album on the dining room table waiting for her to see the contents. I was eager to pass it to her, so she could begin to see how it came to be that four little ladies could be created from something that had gone so wicked. It was going to be also be my excuse to once again look at the memories that I had boxed away within these photographs. I was also hoping that revealing this side of me would not cause me to lose control of my emotions. Nona began to ask, "Empress, tell me about that the wedding day."

I began to gulp and slowly recalled the many feelings I had, as opposed to actual events I remembered at first. I resigned to begin with the arrival of the ladies at my mother's house. As the pictures in my wedding album were in sequential order, it was not hard to recall the many events after some time of gathering my thoughts. After not to long, it became much easier for me to talk about that day. I began to rap and sing, "It was all a dream, I used to read Word-Up Magazine—" she busts out laughing, commenting that I'm so funny and that I often reminded her of her older sister that she would give her life for.

As I began to get serious, I could feel a sense of sadness come over me and the reality was that I was run over by my emotions. "I loved him. I would have done anything for him, Nona, but the problem was he wasn't willing to do the same for me. We had the best wedding that day, and the marriage was very nice for a while."

"Tell me more, Empress. You know I'm planning my wedding now, and I want to hear about how you planed yours; these pictures are so lovely; you look like a Barbie doll. And Destiney is definitely your twin, Sis."

"Well as the ladies began to arrive at my mother's house, she welcomed everyone and offered them breakfast and tea. We continued laughing and talking for a little while waiting for some of the others to arrive, including the makeup lady that I hired to do the makeup for the girls and myself. At the same time, the photographer was set to arrive to begin the process of recording the history that was about to go down." I began to unravel the events of that day. "It was a hectic day, Nona, but it had to be my day, so I was determined to make it work."

"There are many signs in life, some that you may not like. You don't have to be a Christian to call on Jah's name. Hold up your head my brothers, be conscious my sisters and by your works you shall surely be paid—" I sat on the sofa next to her, singing the tunes that come out of my new speaker tower.

Everyone thought we were the perfect couple and most people could not believe it when I left, no one would ever image that there could have ever been any valid reasons for me to leave. I was so consumed with making everything look good. I forgot to make sure it was all really good in my heart. There were so many secrets, lies, promises, things that were never said, places we never went, attempts that were forgotten and times I wanted out way before I left. The good days blinded me and kept me living a promise that one day things would be better, that one day the person that I married would become the person I needed him to be, but the reality was he never knew what I wanted because he never looked up nor down for that matter.

"Who is this lady, in the maroon dress," Nona asked.

"It's my mother-in-law; why do you ask?"

"In every single picture, she has a screw face." Nona commented.

"She was highly upset that day because Gary's father embarrassed the family by not showing up to his son's wedding. Would you believe that he died the next year on that same day, Nona? He was upset because Gary refused to ride to the church with him on the wedding day instead. Gary wanted to take a limo with his friends as they customarily do in America. Gary was breaking some Nali tradition that made him so upset that he refused to attend the wedding, and I liked his father Nona." For the entire time, I was married to Gary; that was her attitude; she didn't smile nor mingled. My mother would invite her to our family functions; not only would she not show up, but when she had functions, she never invited my mother over. That was my mother-in-law! A real bitch! The fact is I never had any respect for her; she never did anything to help my family grow as a united family. As a matter of fact, I believed she did everything in her power to put wedges in my marriage." I announced to Nona hoping that she would understand that no woman should have to be so degraded by another.

Dear Diary:

Today was one of those days I hope to forget real soon. I was sitting in the dark today with the girls because our lights were turned off again. I had to dip to the bedroom so that they would not see me crying. I have been crying myself to sleep for the past two days, thinking how I am I going to make it to work when I don't have any money for gas for even my car. how am I supposed to get to work?

I called Gary and asked if he could send us a couple of dollars because I was about to lose my electricity, but he said that he could not help us out this time. The girls just got back from visiting with him, so I did not get any money from him this month yet. It is so ridiculous that he doesn't send any support for them when they are with him, but he refuses to understand that their expenses do not stop when they visit with him. I was crying when I was on the phone with him. It was so bad that he called Harmony and told her that I was talking like I was going to hurt myself.

I would NEVER kill myself. I LOVE my children to much. I am very depressed though and often get jealous to hear that Gary is dating Jelana. His seeming happiness irks me. I wish I could find me somebody—not these ass clowns, Carlos or Raymond—users that they are.

Anyway, I'm just going to wait around. It'll soon get dark, and we will have to light the candles again, so we can bath. As for dinner, I bought them a pizza from Little Arcs. I didn't eat cause it wasn't enough really, but the kids are so brave, and they didn't complain one bit. We will all sleep in the living room where I'm going to stay up all night watching them and making sure theses candles don't cause a fire. Perhaps, I'll break down tomorrow and ask my mom for help again.

Empress

***

"Empress are you ok?"

"Yes, Nona, I was just thinking about something from the past. Girl, my wedding day was awesome, we had almost 250 people there. It was a lot of fun. Remind me to tell you about Peter Gaye. Anyway, I was so excited for this day. One of my friends and I were getting married the same month, so we did a lot of planning together. In the end, that friend and I stopped talking because she felt I did not give her enough attention. The truth is, I've lost a lot of friends over the years, Nona, because I thought that to focus on my family, I needed to give my family all of my time. I know. Don't ask." I was twenty-two years old when I got married. To this day, I was still very naïve because I never had a dating life. But I pray that God will open my eyes soon.

I later learned giving up your friends doesn't necessarily make you a better wife or mother, and to me, it was not true at all; you don't have to give up your friends to gain your family, at least not in every case. Sometimes real friends can be there to remind you of who you really are!

"Your dress is absolutely gorgeous, Empress; do you still have it?" asked Nona.

"Yes, I do. I am saving it for Destiney; she loves the fact that I have it there for her. My mother has been keeping it for me since I moved to Florida. I looked at it this summer and sent a picture of it to Destiney. She said that she and Vanessa got into an argument about who was going to actually get it."

"Yeah, Sis, that dress, these pictures, and my children are the only things left from that fourteen-year marriage. I gave it my all, but I wasn't about to let this marriage rob me of any more time."

The wedding day, on the other hand, was magical. Although there were obvious signs that things were not going to be a bed of roses. In my head, I am more than a million miles away.

"How can you tell me who is supposed to be in my wedding party?" I'm screaming at Gary.

"I have no respect for your cousin anymore, and I do not want her in my wedding party. These women are supposed to be my best friends. She betrayed me," I replied.

"What are you talking about, Empress, come on, this is childish."

"You will never know it feels. I just called Flavia; she said she was home alone." I'm screaming now.

"You just told me that Keyshana's mom was over Flavia's house when you got there. How is Flavia my friend? And she's best friends with your baby mama? I cannot trust her, and I don't want her in my wedding."

"Empress, please, she's my cousin, and she already bought her dress, can you do it for me, please?"

I looked into his eyes, and my mouth says "okay."

I quickly return to the conversation of the wedding day that Nona and I was having.

"The wedding day was like a movie, Nona, but it was my wedding, and I had a lot of fun. It was like a movie, and I was the star of the show. And no matter how things seemed the pictures showed so much. The faces, the expressions, the shoes that didn't match, the cakes that were ordered, the flowers that were chosen, the DJ that kept everyone dancing, oh yeah, and then there was Peter Gaye.

So, I was getting ready the throw the bouquet, and all the ladies get up to get in place, preparing themselves to catch the bouquet. Unbeknown to me, my little cousin-in-law joined the ranks. Now the men are patiently waiting to see who Neil's brother Egor will get to put the garter on. I threw the bouquet, and Peter Gaye catches it, when he realized it's a twelve-year-old, he demanded a redo; it was hilarious. Obviously, he wanted to be nasty and couldn't with this little girl. By the way today, Peter Gaye and I are the best of friends. After the second toss, Donna catches it. Boy did the party take a different mood. Egor used his mouth to put the garter on Donna's leg. It was quite the scene," I reminisced while I showed Nona the picture of that event in the album.

"Empress, it sounds like you had a lot of fun." Nona commented. "Yes, I did, Sis." I nodded.

"Do you see this picture?" I pointed to one where all the groomsmen were holding me up. Well, Gary was so mad that I allowed that picture to be taken. He said that the men were groping my ass while the photographer was taking the picture. We both laughed. Nona commented, "Are you serious?" Sadly, I replied "Yes."

"And in this picture, you can see the rum cake that was made especially for me by Mrs. Gravesend, my former neighbor. Mrs. Gravesend took swatches of my girls' dresses and made the dresses on the dolls on the cakes; aren't they classy?" I suggested. "It is beautiful, Empress; wait you had two cakes?" Nona asked. "Yes, Nona," I replied.

"Yes, boo, it is customary that you also offer sponge cake to the guest that do not use rum." I informed her.

"If I had to do it over, I would still have wanted the storybook wedding day that I had. My mom was so proud, and my dad was so happy to see that I was happy. My family always looked up to me for being married, responsible, and tidy with my children and home. There was just one problem, Sis, I was unhappy."

I lived my days, day in and out trying to be someone, but I wasn't happy. I wanted so much to remain loyal and true to the man that I had vowed my life to. I hoped that we could grow old together and see our children's children together. I wanted so much. I gave so much. I hoped, dreamed, cried, I lived, but I wasn't living; I was surviving.

In retrospect, the biggest mistake I made was thinking that I could pretend that all was well and never being brave enough to stand up for what I wanted. I tried to make other people proud and happy and lost myself on the way. I know now where I want to be in life and saw that we, he and I, were not really interested in achieving the same types of dreams. I wanted so badly to remain with my husband and forgot to remain true to myself. And while I so want to blame it all on his selfishness, I knew that I could not continue to live with animosity and disgust. And at some point, I must take responsibility for allowing things to become as they were. For no one can treat you in a way you do not accept; if you do not accept it, then they cannot perform the act.

<o>

Dear Diary:

You would not believe it! I think that there is an infestation of mice in the house. I woke up and went into the cabinets and all the things I just brought from BJ's had mice holes in it. There were mice droppings all over the floor, in the cabinet. I was so upset. I talked to Gary about the situation; guess who cleaned up the mess. I asked him if he could give me some money to replace the items, and he told me that things are real tight for him right now.

I spent the good part of this cold day cleaning up and looking for big plastic or metal containers that I can keep the food products in because I am afraid that I will go through this again. I could definitely see where the mice were coming in. Perhaps I can put some foil paper in the holes until I can get someone to look at it for me. It is pointless to ask Gary to fix it although he did say that he was going to buy some rat poison.

Once again, we got into an argument about money because I told him that it is ridiculous that I paid for so much. He continued to ask me to do a budget with him, but he never found the time to do it. Then he asked me if I'd rather

34

pay the mortgage, and he pays everything else. I said yes but that never happened either. We are having some financial disagreements quite often. I felt like he just needed to do more. We argued over the fact that he needed to help more in the house as well.

After watching the commercial on TV for the hundredth time, I finally figured out that he was taking Viagra, but I do not know why. It's not like we are sex monkeys or anything. Anyway, I will keep you posted when I find out more. I continued to put the bottle back on the bookshelf where he has it hidden behind the books. I couldn't image why he was keeping something like this from me.

Empress

I cannot express the joy and pride that I had on that day. As my friends and family joined to witness the joining of our unions and families, it seemed as though it was all a show. I could never have imaged that I would be where I am today, sitting in Florida, away from my family and friends. Separated from marriage and raising my children alone. For no one can foresee what will take place after that wedding day. The smiles, the tears of joy, the memories would all fad, but the most important test would be, could you withstand the days when you must take into consideration your mate's feelings? Would you jump over the mountain and remove the burdens of life just to see each other smile? Would you make sacrifices for each other that will stand the test of time? Would love bring you through when there is nothing else? Could you really see each other in pain and know that it is you that have caused such pain?

There are yet no answers to reveal, but the journey of one's course in life will reveal answers that you cannot ignore. Judge not the journeys of others, for one day, their roads may become a part of your life's journey.

For on my wedding day stood a young, beautiful, vibrant, proud woman, a woman of courage, a woman that had long left the scene. At that time, there was a willingness to reveal my innermost secrets and faults and desires to be the wife of my king. I wanted to live in that moment forever. I wanted to stand tall and firmly planted, as long as the days of my life. I never thought that I would choose myself over him nor did I see myself as a single mother, barely surviving. I never saw the signs that were before me. I was blinded by my sight. And now, I am crippled by my love.

PARADISE ISLAND

"Band-Aids don't fix bullet holes. Now we got bad blood."
It was such a lovely day for a wedding. I had spent countless hours preparing by having my dress altered, having my shoes dyed the same color as the dress. I even went to the florist to purchase baby breathe that I put in my hair the morning of the wedding. My girlfriend, Natalie was getting married, and she asked me to be one of her bridesmaids. The bride decided that her bridal party was going to meet at her mother's house to get dressed for the wedding. I never mind going to Natalie's house since growing up, I always adored her mother. After we were all made up in our attire, makeup and accessories, we waited for the limo to take us to the church in Middle Island. Natalie was my longtime friend, and we knew each other from growing up on the block in Gullie. We knew a lot about each other, things others did not know. We held secrets for each other and covered whenever a good excuse was needed. And despite the Crotya/Mahlia friction that often existed in Gullie, we were the best of friends.

While driving to the church, I sat back and listened to the young girls as they told stories about love. And I shared in the stories with pieces of my life that made me the happiest. I shared those parts that I was not ashamed of and those things that made me proud. Of course, I could not help but to think back to my own wedding day where Natalie was also a bridesmaid in my wedding. It appears we were always there to support each other at the most important times in our lives. We continued to share laughter, wine, encouragement, and a bond that often exist with women even though some in the party were just meeting for the first time. It was not much longer until we were to arrive at the church. Natalie looked so beautiful; her dress was pink ordained with lace and tulle, and it was her second marriage, so she wanted to have something nonconventional. She had her dress specifically made for her by a Crotyian designer that her family knew. Natalie was always so proud of her culture and displayed it any chance she could. It was a unique dress, and it fit her body contours perfectly. The bridesmaid dresses also contoured our bodies which was one of my favorite styles since I had always had such pride in my physique. I never was one that worked out, but my family life kept me well in shape. Now having three children, I was happy that my body didn't show many signs of motherhood.

Gary arrived at the church, just as we were marching into the church. I could see him gleaming with pride. He was always saying how beautiful I was, and I knew that he appreciated my natural beauty. I had been letting my hair grow back which made him very happy because he hated when I cut it. At this point, it was flowing down my back, so I had dropped curled it up for the wedding. I used bobby pins to pin up the back of my hair, keeping my back cool. To him, my long hair was my crown, and he just did not support my short hair styles one bit.

Everyone in the church stood up as Natalie prepared to march down the aisle to meet her husband-to-be at the altar. It was a Catholic wedding, so there was some praying on my knees that made me a little uncomfortable, but all in all it was a lovely ceremony. As soon as they were pronounced husband and wife, we got ready to make our way to the reception hall. Having to go back in the limo was going to be fun, and I was looking forward to chilling out with the entire party because the men and women were going to be arriving in the same limo. Natalie and her husband were going to take the other limo to the reception hall, all by themselves.

Marondale, Middle Island, was beautiful at this time of the year with the fresh lawn and budding flowers; it was the perfect place for a wedding reception. After taking pictures, the wedding party began to mingle with the crowd. Sensing that Gary was missing me, I headed over to the table where Natalie sat, Jazmine next to him. They were seemingly engaged in conversation while eating their salads. I wanted to stay and hang out by their table, but the bridal party was sitting together at the dais as it was customary. After a few minutes of small talk, I proceeded to the dais to have dinner. It was a delicious meal, and the hall was decorated just beautifully. Sometime during the reception, the bridal party had taken pictures with the bride and groom on the bridge in the outside garden. I wanted to take that same picture with Gary. I walked over to their table and asked Jazmine if she would take the picture of us, so we walked outside in the lawn, went on the small bridge, and took our picture. A little while after, Jazmine went inside, while Gary and I stayed outside and continued talking.

We reminisced on the good times, bringing up our wedding and talking about how much fun we had too. I asked him if we could try harder than ever to listen to each other and stop yelling at each other especially in front of the children. He asked me what he can do to help. I responded to him, saying to try to be more helpful and romantic. I wanted him to open doors for me, bring me random flowers. I wanted him to take me to clubs and act silly sometimes. I wanted to get out and see the world, and I wanted to do it all with him. He listened that evening, but I do not think he heard one word I said.

We continued celebrating well into the night, at the wedding, eating, drinking, dancing and just having an enjoyable time. After taking a few more pictures with the bride and her new husband, we decided that we were going to start making our way back to Gullie. I told Jazmine that she was going to ride back to Gullie with us, although Gary was a little upset with me because I did not ask him first. The problem was I felt I did not have to ask him to help my sister out by giving her a ride. Jazmine really did not have many options at the wedding for getting back home since Harmony did not attend. The only people Jazmine knew at the wedding were Natalie, Gary, and myself. And while I understood that he wanted to spend time alone with me, I was only offering my sister a ride home not asking her to spend the night at our home. He would often bring up the fact that he believed I was being negatively influenced by Jazmine.

My sister used to spend the night at my house sometimes, but that has not happened in quite some time ever since Gary started giving Jazmine the cold shoulder whenever she came to the house. It has gotten to the point that Jazmine does not really come over to the house anymore when Gary is around. Gary gets made when I go over to see Jazmine at her house which is the house that I grew up in as well, but it's the only way I can get to spend some quality time with my sister. I have even noticed the way Gary acted around my mother had begun to change. Whenever either one of them, Jazmine or my mother, come to the house, he would run upstairs to watch TV instead of watching the large screen TV in the living room. And as much as his family irks my nerves, I would never expect him to alienate his family.

Dear Diary:

Today, I called out from work. Gary has no idea that I did not go to work. Jazmine and I hung out today; its Sister's Day. Sister's Day is a day that we created that we can spend time with each other and just have fun like we used to do. Let's face it; I just did not feel like going to work today. As usual, I made Gary a breakfast sandwich, took the kids to school, and pretended like it was going to be an ordinary day at the office. After, I discussed with him what I was planning on preparing for dinner that evening. I just left!

Once I got to Jazmine's boyfriend's house, I took a nap since they were still sleeping. I was so tired. I kept thinking as I began to fall asleep on their couch. I am working six days a week now and going to school on Sunday, basically all day. It's like I never get a break, so I must take a mini-vacation at my sister's house. Some people would say this is truly pathetic, but this is what I'm doing these days to just try to escape. We ordered Japanese takeout food for lunch and had some drinks. It was then that I admitted to my sister, that I want to go to counseling with Gary. She advised me that I should do what I think is best for myself and my family.

When I came home, Gary asked me how my day was. I just lied and said it was long. I could never admit to him that I spent the day with Jazmine instead of him. But when I stay home with Gary, I wind up washing clothes or dishes, and not really relaxing. Also, I really needed to talk about the feelings I'm having, so I needed a sister day. Jazmine said that for our next sister's day, we are going to Chinatown for lunch, already looking forward to it. I missed having my sister coming around my house, but at least with sister's day, we surely make up for it.

Well, I hear the kids arguing, so let me see what that's about! Talk to you soon!

Empress

"Hi there," says someone at the door.

"May I help you?"

"Yes, I'm here to pick up my daughter; someone called me from the office today to say that she was sick and that someone needed to come and pick her up." I commented to the lady sitting by the desk.

Just as I said that, Ms. Hernandez, principal of PS 109 came out of her office and greeted me with the happiest smile. "Connie, this is one of the most fabulous parents, Ms. Braxton; she is a member of our PTA. Can you please call Ms. Burn's class and have Christiana sent downstairs for early dismissal?"

"Yes, Ms. Hernandez" Connie replied.

It was always a pleasure to go to the children's school. Since I was such an active parent in all the children's' schools, I was always well-respected and appreciated by the school's staffs. Even though I was leaving work again to pick up one of our kids, I was not bothered by that fact. I only worked about twenty minutes driving time from PS 109, so it was most convenient that I would pick up Christiana since she was feeling good. Before leaving the job, I called my AP and told her that I had to go because my daughter got sick. She asked me if I left work for the students and reminded me to sign out before leaving the building.

I was a very huge asset at my job, and I knew it, but I was careful not to take advantage of anyone. Most people had a great deal of respect for me while there were a few that thought I was too young to have so many accomplishments. I was a hardworker and very good at getting people to work with me and delegating responsibilities was hard for me since I was a perfectionist and wanted to do things myself. At the job, I was now fourth-in-line in terms of chain of command. To say that I had a lot of responsibilities was an understatement. Sandy, the principal of the school, was behind me 100 percent all the way in terms of helping me to secure an administration job even telling me when she knew of vacancies. Despite all the support I've received at work, I wanted more.

I finally reached home with Christiana, after taking her straight to the doctor's office. I was exhausted. I decided to pick up all the kids so that I wouldn't have to go back out since the weather was expected to get worse in just a few hours due to the quick plundering temperatures outside. I already knew that Christiana was probably not going to be able to go to school tomorrow since she was very fatigued and febrile. For some reason, she has not gotten better since her last cold and the doctors had been contemplating on increasing her steroids, which I am so against. I decided to phone Gary and asked him if he would be able to stay home with her tomorrow since I had already lost time at work today by leaving early.

As Gary picked up the phone, I began to tell him that Christiana was sick again and that I had left work early and that he would need to take off tomorrow to stay home with. Her fever was still off and on, and the weather was going to be so terrible. I had believed that it was in her best interest to stay at home. Before I could finish my last sentence, he cut me right off stating, "You know I cannot take off work. There is just no way that I can stay home tomorrow. It is the end of the month and it is a busy time of the year and there is no way that I can afford to miss one day this week." That was when I lost all control over my mouth, and for a second, I had become one of those drunken sailors that curse way too much at the docks.

I let off a "what the hell" so loud that I think that the explorers on the moon heard me that day. I could not believe that once again, Gary was acting like it was my responsibility to stay home with the children when they got sick. He was never available to takeoff from work when the children needed someone to stay home with them. I thought it was a fair trade since he did not lose any time like I did just last week when Christina had to go for testing, and I had to takeoff two days in a row from my job. I screamed so loud that I had forgotten we even had neighbors. I was tired of Gary always telling me that he could not takeoff time from his job. Because I was a teacher, he felt that it was easier somehow for me to miss days at work. In addition, since the NYT teachers had a very strong union, he believed that the union would save me if I ever got in trouble for taking off time for my children. The truth was I did not care who was willing to forgive me, I wanted to go to work. I did not want to be the only parent staying home when the kids were sick. Because I only used my sick days for my kids, meant I could use those days for nothing else but to take care of my children, by myself again, even if I were ill. Gary was not willing to takeoff from his job, ever. I think he thought it was a part of motherhood, so what then is part of fatherhood?

There was nothing that I wasn't willing to do for my children but since Christiana had been diagnosed with the same blood disorder as Destiney, the amount of time spent in the hospitals, doctor offices, social offices, etc. were now doubled, and it had all really taken a toll on my patience. I was the only one that sacrificed these days for the children, and it was adding to the frustration that I was feeling in my marriage at this time.

⚬⊙⚬

Dear Diary:

Today I received notification from the Make-a-Wish Foundation, and they are going to grant Destiney's wish, to go on a Disney Cruise. I am so happy. The HEMOC team of Riley's Hospital is really awesome. They always seem to have some kind of little way of trying to let us see that despite the way the hospital looks, they are really trying to give our children the best medical care. I am forever grateful to them for sending us to IH (Institute of Health) where they basically saved Christina's and Destiney's life. They were diligent enough to seek professionals that were more skilled about their disorder, ALPS, since nothing they were doing at the time was improving the children's' quality of health.

We are going to be gone for ten-full days, and everything is included. What can be better for our family at this time? We don't have to worry about the airfare, or paying for the actual cruise, and we're also docking in the Bahamas. Guess what? They are even providing pocket money and a limo ride to the airport. The children are going to be so excited. I remembered when the ladies from Make-A-Wish came to this house to interview us to see if we were real I guess. Next thing you know, we were getting invited to all kinds of events, now this. I just can't wait.

I am really looking forward to spending this time with the family. We have been going through a lot lately with the girls being constantly sick. The doctors still didn't know if there is a cure for this disease. I have been to so many appointments lately. I'm just drained. I really needed this, so do the children. I hope this will help us because paradise seems so far away now.

Empress

                        ↄ◦ↄ

It was raining so hard outside, and I just wish this man would hurry up and come back home so I wouldn't have to rush to meet the girls in the city. Some of my coworkers decided we were going to go out and help Asia celebrate her birthday. We had all slowly become friends although some of the girls were not as close as others. I had been looking forward to going out and hanging out tonight. I was dressed for the last thirty minutes now, and I was started to get quite impatient. It seemed like every time I wanted to go somewhere, Gary always had to go out first and somehow, I would have to wait on him. It never really seemed to matter where I was going. I seemingly had to wait on him if I did not want to leave the kids at home alone since they were still so young.

Leaving the kids at home alone was not an option at this point, so I proceeded to pick up my phone and started dialing his phone number. As I picked up the phone to call, I could hear the keys rustling at the front door. The anger that was boiling up was surely about to come out. I resisted the urge to argue and proceeded to walk right out the door without saying one word. As I got in my car, I began to swell up and cry. I drove to the end of the block, parked the car, and just let it out, a cry that to this day I can still remember. I couldn't image why he was treating me like this, instead of encouraging me to take it easy and just relax sometimes he just constantly kept doing things to get me upset. I remembered thinking, I never cried so much in my life.

I sat in my car although it was cold outside, despite that fact that I'm late, pondering life. How did I get here? When did it start to go bad? Are we going apart? Can we fix this? Whose happiness was I looking to save? I had no answers, and this made me very sad. Why was this happening to me? I tried to be the best wife and mother and slowly everything was fallen apart. I was certain that we were going to make this work. I could see the faces of the children. They are so pretty, so smart, so deserving yet was I teaching them the right lessons? I had so many decisions to make! I had so many thoughts! First, I had put my car in drive and get myself out of this parking space. My friends were waiting, and I did not want to let them down either!

As I reached to the city, the excitement of the atmosphere filled my soul, and I once again was able to relax. I saw the sign "HIPS" and knew that I was in the right place. It was going to be so exciting to be hanging out with the girls, having some food and drinks and watching the show of transvestite men lip-syncing. It was a packed house, and everyone was having such a fun time. We were there for about two hours when my phone started vibrating; it was Gary. He was texting me to find out what time I was coming home. I ignored his text, yet he continued. After about three texts, I decided to ask him why he needed to know what time I was coming home. Apparently, his friend was having a house party, and he was wondering if I would be home in time for him to go for a little while. After hearing that was the reason for the texts, I continued ignoring it and proceeded to turn off my phone.

Dear Diary:

I am so excited to see where this vacation is going to take us. I have planned the perfect get-a-way for Gary and me to the Dominican Republic, Punta Cana. I left all the all-inclusive plans to the same travel agent that planned our trip to Nali. The place is supposed to be really nice. I even had Lorna teach me some things to say in their dialect of Spanish when I get there.

I hope that this vacation will bring Gary and I closer together because right now, everything seems to be falling apart. I hope that this paradise vacation will remind us of the hopes and dreams that we once shared about our future. I hope that we will be renewed, refreshed, and redefined. I need this to work! If it doesn't, I don't know what else I'm going to do. The counselor thinks it's a great idea to get away and spend time with each other. Maybe we can talk about things and make better resolutions. Of course, I'm taking you with me, so I'll keep you posted.

Empress

After a rather long plane ride including a mini plane, we finally arrived in Punta Cana. This place was just what I needed. It was beautiful; the food was authentic; and the smell of the Caribbean Sea made me feel very much at home in Mahlia. We traveled by chartered bus to our resort which was in a quite isolated location and seemingly host to many couples. We checked in and proceeded straight to the room. The standing shower, mini bar, Jacuzzi, canopy bed, and fruit basket were an instant reminder that we were far from home. Not having cell phone access was a welcome plea for quiet time for both of us. We immediately put our luggage down and walked toward the balcony where we could hear the laughter of people and the melodies of the live band. The air was filled with the aroma of baked goods, and we were eager to see what was going on around the resort.

We turned on the TV and watched the resort station to hear about the activities that were to take place during the week that we were visiting. And after listening to the many options, we decided that we were going to go to dinner and dancing for the first evening of our vacation. It was also our wedding anniversary, so we were given complimentary bottles of wine and flowers by the resort. It was a lovely set up but before I could have a really enjoyable time I had to call my mom and make sure the children were alright.

"Hey, Mom, how are the children? We made it safely, and everything's seems to be just fine. Can I speak my little baby please?" I said to my mom, trying so hard to keep the conversation short since we are using the resort phone to make this call. "All the children are doing great. They are already asking about you, of course. Hold on, I'm going to give Dahlia the phone and see if she says anything?" Mom replied. "Hi, Baby Girl, how are... Mom loves you... I see you soon..." I patiently said as I hoped that she speaks but she's only one, so she really does not say much.

My mother returned to the phone after I now have spoken to all the kids, and not once does Gary asked to speak to them. I told the kids that their dad says hi and then hanged the phone up. I proceeded to walk back on the balcony where Gary was sitting listening to the vibes. "I thought you were coming in the room to come and speak to the children" I said to him. "I know you would tell them I said hi, and we will talk to them again before we leave" he said. I couldn't help thinking *what is wrong with this man? how long does it take to say hi?* But I was determined not to bring up any negative energy this week.

I continued talking about the plans for the evening which included dinner at the resort's Italian restaurant and dancing at the local night club. We decided that before getting ready for the evening, we would go grab a snack from the cantina downstairs, a drink from the bar, and sit out a few minutes by the pool. I watched the behavior of the other couples at the resort; they were holding hands, constantly kissing, gazing into each other eyes, and seemingly so into their partners that they never even saw me staring. We were not acting like those couples I watched, instead we acted more as if traveling partners who did this often. Gary and I were seemingly friends, but the romance that was supposed to resonate from the setting was not apparent for us. We were among the few "interesting couples" that were here, interesting in the sense that we weren't romantic.

After gallivanting about the resort, we decided to head back to our suite. Once there, I put the radio on and listened to the merengue that was playing. In many ways, it reminded me of reggae, and it was a definite familiar sound having arrived from Gullie. I began to open the suitcase to search for the desired vogue for the evening. I was satisfied with my choice and decided that I was going to take a shower. There were so many little trial bottles in the bathroom, lotion, shampoo, toothpaste, etc. Each one smelled like a spring garden. I gathered my towel and washcloth and closed the shower door behind me. As I turned on the water, the tears began to stream faster than the water. All at once, I could see eleven years of my life. I see each picture reel-to-reel. I just did not want to continue crying.

How could I be on paradise island and still feel like so sad, so lost, so confused? When did I forget who I was? What fantasy island was I living in? How could I expect things to change with a person that felt there was nothing to change? I mean Gary actually told me there was nothing more he could do. I saw myself taking out the garbage every Wednesday and Saturday, washing the kitchen and dining room floors, spending most waking hours with the children alone. I saw myself once again cooking and wondering if Gary was going to eat after coming in from being on the road, and yes, I saw myself unhappy forever. And yes, that's why I cried that day and most days after that.

Dear Diary:

I went horseback riding today on the beach in Punta Cana. I can't tell you the last time I did that. At first, I had to really talk myself into going, but Gary planned this day trip, so I just went with it, and I am so glad I did. After horse backing, we went on a boat ride where we ended off at a ranch where we had lunch. It was the best Dominican food I had since we have been here.

Tomorrow, I want to go into the town and buy some empanadas and souvenirs. Gary bought me this outfit from the gift shop; it's really cute, and he has been trying so hard to be nice. I am trying to get it together and accept his kind gestures!

The children are all well so far. We only have two days left here. I am going continue to enjoy this lovely time away and do the best that I can to work with Gary on his attitude toward our family and his role as a man. I hope this trip will be all that I need it to be, two days left. Do you think it's possible that we grew apart? I mean, I can honestly say that I grew up since we have been married, and I got more educated about the world; and he kind of stayed where he's been since I met him. I don't know the answer; it's just something I thought about!

Anyway, got to go to bed early because we are going on a tour of the island in the morning, and we must be downstairs for the bus quite early. Looking forward to seeing more. I even hear that they grow ackee here. Hopefully I will see some ackee on the tour tomorrow!

Empress

When you think you will never win, think again, but understand that you must be patient. Always live good, walk straight, and treat people they way you want them to treat you. I never really comprehended those morals until years late; for example, when Gary wind up paying me back for some of those sick days I took for the children after all. I never wanted him to take every sick day, just share in the responsibility. I presented a bill from NYTDOE (New Texas City Department of Education) in court five years later. You see, NYTDOE had paid me for thirteen days more than they should have, due to sick days I had taken that I did not really have. It was during the final decree that the judge ordered Gary to pay for half of these and all marital expenses that I was burdened with for so long. I bet Gary wished he had taken some sick days that day! Be strong, your day is coming.

THREE'S A CROWD

My sister was in town visiting again. Somehow, she had made it to Florida eleven times since I had moved here some eight months ago. She was my everything, and I was so happy that she was able to come down here so often because I really missed my sisters more than anything else that I had left behind in New Texas. The one thing I did not miss was the cold weather, and it was becoming colder in New Texas, so Jazmine decided that she was going to escape the weather by coming for another visit. She was single and kid-free, so traveling was something that she really enjoyed. It was the part of her that I always admired, the part that was able to go where ever she wanted whenever she could.

Whenever she came down, we would always make it to the club, and I would always have such a great time while she was here. One thing she always did during her visits was to buy the children some Pancake House and take them to the beach. Since I really did not like going to the beach, the kids always looked forward to when she took them. The times that she came down, she always brought us some groceries, snacks, and even some kind of fish and treats from Chinatown. There were these hotdog snacks from Chinatown that were my favorite and she always made sure she brought some with her. Despite our age difference, she is seven years younger; we were the best of friends; being sisters was just a bonus. So often, we would find ourselves chatting at 5:00 am about the various events of our lives. We had a bond that most people wish they could have.

There were many things people did not know about my sister, Jazmine. She was tall and rarely smiled on the streets; she didn't hold her tongue though when it came to be stating how she felt about things. People saw that side, the side that said, "You betta not fuck with me." But she did not often show her caring side, the side of her that she would do anything for you. I knew the latter side in many forms; when I did not have groceries or money for gas, she would give it to me; when I could not afford to go to Mahlia, she paid for my entire vacation and gave me pocket money too. She hurled groceries in her suitcase and made sure my children had money for lunch, and each time she visited, she always gave the girls and I something to remind us how much she loved us. Now there were many reasons why we became so close, but it was mostly because I was raising her while my mom was working. As Jazmine grew up, my mom became a single parent, and I spent so much time taking care of Jazmine and so we developed a natural bond that threatened most people who wanted to become a part of our circle. And while I loved my other sisters dearly, our bond was quite unique.

I talked to her about everything and felt that she really understood the things that I talked to her about. While she was younger than me, I still felt that connection that made us a true unit.

"Empress, I'm about to take the kids to the beach."

"Ok, Sis, thanks. I'm about to take a nap" I said.

"You guys can expect dinner when you come back, I'm about to fry some chicken and make some chips." I stated. "Make sure you take the beach toys," I reminded her as she was about to take my car and headed out the door.

The sky was looking a little gray but that never stopped Jazmine from taking the kids to the beach. Even in New Texas, she would take them to Crystal Beach in the summertime. Sometimes she would buy the kids pizza or KFC and have a beach picnic. And after a while in my deep thought, she was gone, I would always nap once she left, after taking a deep breath.

As the car drove out of the driveway, I could hear the girls singing to the tunes in the car. It always made me smile to hear them singing reggae and wanting to know about my family's adventures in Mahlia. I had taken the girls to Mahlia the summer before moving to Florida, and they were so eager to return. They talked about their experiences of that summer as if they had been there a lifetime.

The best part of it all for them was that they were able to experience Mahlia with their cousins and aunts. Being together in Mahlia that summer was an awesome experience one that the children would not soon forget.

I began to think about that trip to Mahlia and realized that it was a culminating excursion that sealed the end my marriage. It was the best trip of my life, and there were many reasons why I would never be able to forget that experience.

As usual, I began to lay down and hope that I would soon fall asleep. I had been suffering from insomnia now for almost a year and had decided that since I wasn't going to fall asleep for now, that I might as well write in my journal.

Dear Diary:

Today, Jazmine took the kids to the beach. Believe it or not, she's here again. We were just talking about the good old days in New Texas when we would have our sister's days. She reminded me of the time that she asked Gary to take the kids to the beach and he told her no because he felt that she was too irresponsible. We both laughed because we both knew that she was a certified life guard.

I called Gary while Jazmine took the kids out. I wanted to see what he was doing and if he was still planning on coming down to get the kids for their Christmas vacation. We began talking, and I asked him about Jelana. I asked him if he loved her. He told me yes and that she had never did anything to him so there was no reason for him to be cruel to her. I asked him if he knew when he met her that he loved her, and he said no. I hated her, and the sad part is she really thinks he loves her. If only she knew about the babysitter Rosalie that's always at his house.

The one thing I felt confident was that my husband never cheated on me, but as I reflect on the Viagra, I am not so sure. I can never admit, at least for now, that I slept with Gary since I moved to Florida because it was so horrible that I hope to forget it. I don't know really what possessed me to ever sleep with him other than loneliness and a longing for a man that truly knows me. I will never again sleep with him especially now that he has these worthless women in his life. I think the truth is I'm just jealous that he has someone that he loves, and I do not. The funny thing Carlos means nothing to me, yet I pretended like he does just to forget the loneliness. And while I know Carlos can never be mine and Gary can never be mine again, I needed to do more about forgetting them both.

Anyway, I am trying to lie down now, so I'll write back to you later.

Empress

As I lay down, I could hear the pitter-patter on the window and realized that it had begun to rain. The rain used to make me so nervous and scared. I could hardly sleep through it as a young child. As I got older however, it became my favorite type of weather. What once brought fear to me was now cleansing me and somehow making me whole again.

Ring Ring. The alarm went off on my phone prompting me to get up. It had been two hours since the kids have left and now it is time that I get up and start dinner. As I looked outside, I could see that the rain had stopped and that the sun had come back out. It was an event that happened often in Florida whereas it would rain suddenly and then stop just as soon. I loved it; it reminded me so much of Mahlia, and I could not wait to make a return to Mahlia.

Jose had been calling me all day wanting to know when I was returning to Mahlia. The truth was that I missed the attention that he gave me, but I knew as well as he that we could never be a real couple as there was no potential in that relationship. I had a lot of fun sporting with him the summer before moving to Florida, but I had no intentions of being with him. He however was eager to come to America and somehow thought I was going to help him to get here. While he will always special to me as he was the first man that I was with after giving up on my marriage, he was not the true one for me. As I reflected for a moment, it made me sad that I had so easily succumbed to loneliness.

I hid away the hurt of what I had experienced with my husband by dealing with Jose; but I had selfishly allowed him to think that the possibilities were endless when we were together. He was too young for me, and the truth was that I could not allow him to base his life on a woman who never wanted to have any more children. Nor could I allow him to believe that I could love another man at this very moment. My heart was so shattered; never in a million years would I believe that my husband would ever choose another woman over me. But the truth was I made the choice a long time ago to give up on the marriage, and there was no way that our relationship would ever be the same. At that very moment, I realized that I would never again try to rekindle a relationship that I was not happy with in the first place. And the bigger question was, what did I think could possibly change after thirteen years of trying? Was it that I wanted Gary or was it that I did not want him to be happy, while I was not?

I found myself still sitting on the edge of the bed thinking about what Jelana told me just a few months ago during a Facebook battle. "You are nothing but a baby factory." Jelana said to me. It really hurt me knowing that Gary had supported her statement to me, saying that we were arguing and according to him that's what people say to one another during an argument at times, hurtful things. I remembered thinking, *is this guy serious? who disses their baby mama and gets away with it? A punk, that's who,* that was the only response I could think of. Yeah, I was done, and despite the loneliness, I needed to do things differently. I wiped the tears from my eyes and proceeded toward the kitchen, finally.

Opening the refrigerator was something I hated to do because it often reminded of all the things that were missing in my life. I had really wanted to make some oxtail and rice and peas this weekend, but I didn't have enough money to buy it. My kids were always so patient, they never really complained about the no-frills groceries that I so often had to buy. We often ate chicken and turkey wings mostly because it was the cheapest thing to buy. I had often thought about all the food and snacks that once overcrowded my pantry in Gullie. I wished so often that I could just go to BJ's like I used to and buy the snacks that the kids loved. I knew that I had to fry this chicken, so I started to pour the oil into the pan that I had warming on the stove.

As the oil started to crackle, I prepared the batter that I was using after egg washing the chicken. I started to flour the chicken and placed the pieces into the popping oil. It smelled so good. I was so blessed to be able to cook for my family. I knew that although I wished that I could treat them to takeout more often, home-cooked food was better for their health. I began turning the chicken, taking out those pieces that had now become golden brown. While that was frying, I prepared another pan to fry French fries that I had pur-chased at the Dollar Tree. My kids love French fries, and they were never disappointed when I made them.

The food was finally prepared, and it was now cooling on the counter awaiting the return of my family. I scurried to the bathroom in the hopes to steal another few quiet moments whereas I could get a quick quiet shower. As soon as I got into the shower, the phone rang. On the other end was Danielle calling to tell me that there was going to be a hot party tonight that she and the girls were attending. She was inviting Jazmine and I to join the celebrations later that eve-ning. We had agreed to meet at about 11:00 am, so I already knew that meant at least two hours later would be the actual time that we would meet up.

Jazmine and the kids had finally reached home which meant that I had to start the children bathing and washing their hair. It was four of them, so bathing was always a busy time for me. While I was bathing Chrissy in one bathroom, Destiney was bathing in the other, and because these two children always seemed to get sick, I always let them bathe first so that they could dry their hair and hopefully prevent any colds. Vanessa and Dahlia were eating their food while the others were bathing; it was quite a hectic hour. At the same time, Jazmine was in the backyard preparing a fire in the firepit. Jazmine was truly free spirited and needed no occasion to begin celebrating life.

After finally finishing drying everyone's hair, I was finally free to sit and chat with my sister for a while. We seemed to talk about everything, but I wanted to especially make clear that I was intending to go out tonight, and I was most confident that she would want to join in. Due to the fact that I often flaked on club plans, I had to make sure she knew that I was truly going out tonight. The Riders Club was one of our favorite Friday night hangout spots, and Danielle's friend was having a party tonight. We had finally discussed our outfits when I noticed that it was almost 8:00 pm; this made me happy because the children were usually in their beds by 9:00–9:30 pm. I started to go back upstairs to check on the children when I peeked in on the little kids, and they were already knocked out, fast asleep. Vanessa was in her bed, and Destiney was on her iPad, of course. The children were exhausted by the events at the beach which was perfect for me. The faster they fell asleep; the sooner I could prepare for my night out.

As the day became night, Jazmine and I prepared to lay down for an hour before preparing for the party.

⌇⊙⌇

Dear Diary:

    I miss my sister already; it has been a week since she left, and it feels like an eternity.

Raymond called me again; he seems nice. I still can't believe how drunk I was at the club the other night. He said that he doesn't think that I'm a slut just because I was acting up. He's married, another one; what's with me and these married men? At this point though, I really don't care, and I'm just out to have my fun.

I met him the other day at his job; he's truck driver. It was weird and so out of character for me, but we fucked in the truck. I'm so crazy. The truth is, fuck it, it's what I wanted to do, so I did it. I'm living the life. He said that he was going to get my car looked at this weekend, so we'll see.

He's calling me now. I'm going to call him back in a moment. We are supposed to be going to a party this weekend coming up. I don't know how these married men do it. I would have fucked up my husband something bad.

Anyway, all is well for now, I guess.

Empress

Carlos was knocking at my door again saying that he wanted to spend time with me. Even though he told me he was coming by yesterday and didn't, I tried not to seem upset. The truth was that I could only really spend time with him when he was available; this was mostly because he was living with his wife's family while he was living in Florida while going to school. Knowing everything I did about him, I liked him anyway, and I knew he was using me but still, I often felt a love for him. I did not actually love him or like how he treated me, but I certainly had love for him that was hard to explain to others. We were silly together; he was younger than me and had an energy that was magnetic. He was helpful around the house and checked on me as often as he could. Carlos was so sneaky though.

I knew that I was not the only one he was cheating on with, but I still didn't care. I often found myself jealous when I knew he had to spend time with his wife. I knew that this relationship was toxic, but still, I like him.

Carlos was wild and free at least when he was with me. He was careful where he took me, but we were still able to go places together. He was a lady's man, a charmer, and was able to charm his way into spending the night once again at my house. He had brought pizza and chicken wings with him and said that tonight, we would spend the night talking and fucking, which we did. He brought out my wild side, one that had never been explored when I was married. I didn't care that I knew he was poison. The funny thing was that he didn't know about Raymond, and I pretended that I had to hide it from Carlos. I never admitted to Carlos that I was a cheater and user like he was. He always thought that he was the only one that I was dealing with at that time. That was the way I needed it to be, at least so I thought.

I was growing tired of giving all of me and getting nothing to men that never really gave a damn to me. I had confided with my friend, Neville, that I was having an affair with a married man. I never really admitted that it was more than one married man. Although we were only friends, I never wanted him to think badly of me. He would often tell me that I was too good for that type of relationship and that there was no reason to accept that behavior. Neville and I often talked about a lot of things. We were just friends; we spoke on the phone; and he would text me and occasionally invite me out to support one of his lacrosse events. We had spent many hours learning about each other's current relationships and gave each other countless words of advice. But I respected his opinion and being that I really didn't have any homeboys in Florida, he quickly became one.

I had invited Neville to attend the pool party that I had for Asia and I in June of this year, but he was unable to attend. He had never actually been to my house, and since we had not met too long ago, we were now getting to know about each other. I was contented having him as my homeboy; after all, I needed someone to talk to that was down to earth and a male, who I wasn't fucking. I had many male friends like this in Gullie, so I knew that this type of boy/girl relationship was possible. He was cool, and for now, that's how it was going to be. And furthermore, I didn't need any more mates in my life, at least for now. I never made any effort to get to know anyone in a personal way, so I felt that Neville and I had a special bond.

The night was somehow getting cooler, and I never thought that Florida's temperatures could dip so suddenly; apparently, we were having what the locals called, a cold front. It wasn't that cold for a New Texan, but we were certainly not expecting the weather to become so chilly. Destiney was coughing a lot, and I had heard her complaining about her stomach hurting her. While she looked a little pale, she acted as if she was having some cramps or possible some constipation. Despite the fact that she complained of being tired, she had often "faked" being sick, so it was a little hard to gage with her. I went upstairs to see if she woke up from her third nap today. I always worry about the children, especially having experienced what we did some years ago at IH. I had constantly looked at her eyes, trying to see if I saw any signs of distress which I learned about at IH. I did not see any real signs in my opinion, so I really thought she was okay.

The next day for the first time, Neville had invited me to come over to his house and watch TV with him and talk. Even though I knew all about his current girlfriend, I called him back and told him that I would be over soon. I quickly went to take a shower and put on some clothes. It was already getting late and the little kids were fast asleep. I could hear Destiney on the phone with her father, asking her where I was going. I continued to turn off the lights in the little kids' room and go to check on Vanessa in her room. Finally, I went to Destiney and asked her if she was feeling a little better since I had given her some Aleve and Gas Relief earlier. She assured me that she was fine. I told her that I was going out for a while and that tomorrow if she was still feeling bad, we would go to the Urgent Care Center around the block from the house. I reminded her that she could call me anytime while I was out.

I continued down the stairs and headed to my room to grab my purse and spray some perfume on before getting in my car. I was so excited almost nervous not knowing what to really expect. I put the radio on and blasted my favorite reggae CD, and at every light, I looked in the mirror to see if I looked fine. Neville only lived ten minutes away from me, yet we did not see each other often outside of work. I had finally reached to his home and waited for him to buzz the gate so that I could drive through the community. It was a lovely community, but at this time of the night, it hardly seemed like the thing I was interested in noticing. Finally arriving to his townhouse, I proceeded to get out the car.

He waited for me outside and hugged me when I arrived. We entered his home whereas I took off my shoes which was my custom when I enter a home. Asking me if I was interested in having a drink, I quickly responded by saying, "Sure." He poured a shot of rum, and we began to sit on the couch and watched the TV. We talked for about half an hour before he asked me if I was interested in going upstairs to which, I answered saying, "Yes." As we walked upstairs, he was playing with me, being silly and telling me how nice I looked in my jeans. I was blushing at this point and feeling a deep sense of happiness. For some reason, I was comfortable and relaxed and wanted to know more about this man. I proceeded to turn off my phone's ringer and laid down next to him in his bed.

Dear Diary:

I never knew that I would be here looking at my daughter, fighting for her life. This is day two that she is in the hospital, intubated, just trying to stay alive. Her lungs were filled with fluid, and the doctors said that she may not pull out of this. I haven't eaten anything since we arrived here. My mom had been at my house with the other kids so that I could spend most of the time with her. The doctors believed that Destiney will be here for quite some time.

I called Gary but haven't been able to reach him; I heard that he has gone to Mahlia to be with Jelana while our daughter is fighting for her life. I am so depressed right now. I even called his grandmother and brother looking for him. The truth was he's been on vacation for about a week, and I bet he would have never thought in a million years that we would be in this situation.

I really don't know what will happen with all of this, but I will keep you posted. It is a very sad time right now. My poor baby; please pray for her.

Empress

✦

It had been some time since I had been to work, and several people had come to the hospital to look for my daughter while she was there. The people that visited with us tried so hard not to act like they were concerned but clearly, they showed signs of panic. In totally, she was intubated for fourteen days and was finally released from the hospital on day twenty. I watched my daughter fight to breathe but survived this tragedy. After reflecting on all the events that occurred in the hospital, as well as watching the other kids truly suffer and worry for their sister, I decided that no matter how much money I was losing by missing so many days I was going to spend the next two days at home with Destiney while she was recovering. I was determined to see her come fully around; although being in a medically induced coma for so many days, she really didn't remember too much of what had taken place. I had gathered my thoughts and went to sit with her at her bed.

While sitting there, we talked about how important it was for her to take her medicine, and although she hated the fact that the medicine was causing her to put on countless pounds, it was an absolute necessity. I assured her that we all rather that she takes her medicine than be in the hospital ever again. I could not stand the thought of losing her, and the thought of such loss often haunted me. I couldn't help but to think about the fact that she was my daughter, my responsibility, and my love, and while I often struggled with them, they edified my life. I would never be the same again if anything was to happen to any of my children. After this experience, I would never forget the look of pain and regret that was in her eyes. At that very moment, every concern for financial stress and marital disputes went right out the window. I never knew before what was most important in life.

LETTERS TO GREENE COUNTY

It was 305 days since I had last seen my friend, and I was truly missing him. We talked on the phone several times, and I had spoken to him more while he was incarcerated than when he wasn't. From January of the previous year when I last slept with him was the last time I had been with a man, it had been a long time. I had gotten too familiar with my toys, and it was becoming quite sad and depressing not having any male human contact. I had not allowed myself any thoughts of another man based on the feelings, conversations, and the letters we exchanged with one another. Whenever a new man approached me, I always acted as if I had a boyfriend, at least that was what I told them. Even before he went in, we never had a relationship other than friends, and sometimes, I wondered if we were really friends. Our friendship was a strange sort, and it was hard to explain to my other friends whenever they asked me; so seldom did I speak of this twisted relationship.

We had started a relationship based on a lie, and I was always told that the way you begin a relationship is the way you end it. From the day I met him, he had been dating a lady named Shirley. He had seemingly had a great relationship with her until one day, she left him after his problems with the law began. Knowing how she treated him, I had always had a dislike for her and wanted Neville to show me the attention he used to show Shirley. Even though I knew he was a cheater, I still desired to be a significant part of his life. I had always wanted to be happy and was looking for it ever since being separated from my now ex-husband. I never met a man that I could be with or pursue in a relationship since being separated since they all seemed to be either married or almost married. I had hoped that Neville and

I would have started a relationship when he came home, but the events after his release were disappointing. It had been all day that I had been expecting to hear from him although I knew that he would be very occupied with the activities of getting situated within society and his family. While I hoped that he would come straight home to me, I knew that in no way shape or form was that going to happen.

Neville had basically lived with his mother all his life, and even when I went over to see him, which was rare, I always asked him if the coast was clear. He had always replied that he was a single man that he did not have anyone to answer to. I knew that he only said that to me because he wished that he had the freedom to move about and do his own thing. I had always imagined that we would one day share some space together although I was unsure how that was to look. There was nothing particularly special about him to me in his looks nor was I at the least interested that he had once played professional lacrosse. He was simple looking, short, slowly balding, and still, I found him to be so sexy. I had hoped for so long that one day, we could get that second chance that was only once in a lifetime, but perhaps, I had read too deep into the calls, the letter, and the messages he sent to me from Greene County.

The last text and video he had sent me before going in had been saved on my phone all this time. I would often replay them to see his face and remember what his voice sounded like when I missed him. My kids would often ask me for him, as he was the only man that they had seen in my house for a very long time. Whenever they asked, I would simply say that he was out of the country doing business. I knew that I was not the only one that missed him, and that when he got out there was going to be a lot of people that would be anxious to see him, but I never expected what actually happened to take place. In my mind, I figured that after his mom, aunt, grandma, and his kids, I would be the next person that Neville would want to see.

I had been writing to him almost weekly, updating him on the local events in my life and telling him how much I missed him that I had been so eager to see him. My last letter to him had taken me some time to write because the letter before that had come back to me, saying addressee unavailable. After speaking with is mom I was convinced that he would soon be coming home, so I began to think about some things that we could do together once he got out. Through his mom, I had learned that there was an app that alerts as to his release date, so I had the app downloaded to my phone. I would often look at the message although it only changed twice since I had installed it to my phone. It was like an obsession knowing about him and just hoping that he was doing alright down where he was. I would also try to speak with his mother at least once a week so that she would not be so lonely since I knew that she really missed having him around her.

To speak to him on the phone, I had to upload money to a phone account. The phone account allowed him to call me. When he first went in, I was struggling so much financially; it was sometimes so hard to make sure there was money on the account. I had always wanted to have money on the account because I never wanted him to try to call me, and there was no money on the account. If there was no money on the account, that would mean he would not be able to call me, and I never wanted that to happen. One time, he called me like four times, and I knew that there was no way that I could put money on the account.

That day, I called his mother and told her to let him know that I was not going to be able to put money on the account for two weeks until I got paid again. When the two weeks came, I immediately put the money on the account, so he could call me, but it actually took him three weeks before I heard from him. He never really knew the struggles I had before going to divorce court. He never knew about my nights without electricity nor my days without lunch money for my kids; he never knew that I waited every day to hear from him, and certainly he never knew that there was so much to tell him, but there was never any time to speak about those things because he was always so busy.

We never had any special times together other than the ones we shared at night when mostly everyone was busy or sleeping. I can remember specifically three times when we were going somewhere in public in the four years that I have known him so far. It has always seemed to me that he did not really want the world to see us together, and that in many ways, I was just a convenience that he only thought about when he was lonely. And that the random texts he sent me were some type of I-feel-sorry-for-you move or something. When I reflected on Neville and I, never have I ever seen anything authentic between us. I don't know why I believed his words, why I ever thought that he would truly want to try to make our relationship work. I don't know. I wanted it to be real so bad that I forgot to see everything else that was fake.

⚬⚬⚬

Dear Diary:

It has been three months since Neville has left, and it seems like forever. You would think that the man was my boyfriend or something, the way I cried today. I tried to go down into Greene County to go and see him and they rejected me because I was wearing sandals. I cried like a baby. After leaving the jail, I just sat in my car for twenty minutes or so and cried. I really wanted to see him. I felt so bad for myself because I had driven so far to look for him. Who would have thought about shoes as being an issue? I have never been to a jail before; how was I to know? After that moment, I got on the phone and called his mom and told her what had happened. I explained that I wanted to surprise him and that I did not know that there was a dress code. She told me to calm down and gather myself and just head back home. I really felt like going to the store and going to buy some shoes but somehow decided against that idea. I had talked with him this evening, and he told me don't worry about it but that he really did not want me to come down there anymore.

If he knew how much I miss him was my only thought at that time. It had been so long since he has been in there; my initial thought was that they were trying to scare him and that he would be out of there in a week or so, but I soon realized that, that was not going to be the case. I really don't know how long they will keep him there, but his mom is trying to make sure he gets the best lawyers, so I'm sure he will be fine. Being that, he had all these high-profile friends. I just knew that one of them would help him get out faster than he was telling me, which he said might be up to three years. Until later, I'm going to write him a letter now.

Empress

His mom and I had become closer as his time passes; our time seemed to go so slowly. We bonded over the fact that we both loved him and that we both really missed him. I would call her making sure she was feeling okay especially since I knew that Neville wasn't around. I tried to be available for her whenever she needed some assistance. His mother had a sweet disposition about her, and I really took well to her spirit. In the summer months, especially when my time had become a little more available, I would take her to her doctor appointments and spend time with her at the house.

Sometimes she would call me, and we would just comfort each other. It was weird because in all the times that I knew Neville prior to him going away, I had never met his mother much less talked to her on the phone, and now we would chitchat like old-time friends. Neville had always spoke very well about his mom, aunt, and grandmother, but I had never been introduced to either one of them per-

sonally by him. He never invited me to attend any of his family functions nor to come to his house while anyone else was around. And
when I thought about how long I've known him, I only met a few of
his friends. The only person he ever introduced me to was his brother
Paul; he even asked me to call for him while he was locked away
once. I guess Neville never knew that I was the same person when he
was locked away as I am now.

It was hard to believe that I had received a letter from him.
He said that he would write me, but I never believed that he would
actually do it. I had not expected it, and the day it came was like the
best day ever for me. It was the day that I believed that everything
that was ever wrong with our relationship could be corrected, that we
could see something positive out of all of this. I held the envelope at
first not knowing it was from Neville. I did not recognize the handwriting on the envelope because honestly, I had never seen his handwriting before. He had never written me a letter nor sent or given
me a card before, nor did he ever write me a note from a sticky pad.

The day I received his letter was the first time he ever took the
time to put his thoughts to paper and shared them with me. I could
still remember that day, the day I received his letter like it was yesterday. I had come home from work just exhausted and fed up with
everything that was going on. I was just so lonely and tired of acting
like there was someone that had found happiness when they were
with me. I opened the mailbox to see that there was an actual letter
in the mailbox that was addressed to me. As soon as I read the return
address and name, I could not wait to open the letter.

I stopped in my steps and read the letter immediately, as I continued to walk back to my house from my mailbox. His words gave
me such courage and hope for a better tomorrow. His letter told me
a story of a man that was tired of what he was experiencing, and he
was so ready to get on his life. In his letter, he made it clear that he
thought about me, that he was grateful that I was supporting him.
He called me his Indian Mahlian Queen and made me feel special
and that there was some tomorrow that was going to be better than
today's present. I was engaged in every single word he wrote. I read
his letter ten times before I had made it back to my room and gently

placed it next to my bed stand. I was honored that he chose to share this part of his life with me and that he was revealing himself to me. I felt special by that.

I was encouraged that maybe somewhere, there was going to be some type of celebration or at least excitement when he got home. I left that letter there, right where I had placed it; and every time I missed him, I read that letter and looked at the only picture of him that I had, that he had returned to me with his letter like I had asked him to. I hoped that when he finally got out, I was going to be one of those people he would want to see.

The app alert had finally updated indicating that Neville's new release date was going to be less than a month away now. I had not spoken to him for a while, four months to be exact, because the state had moved him again since his final hearing. At this point, he was only allowed to make phone calls to one phone number, and he made those calls to his grandmother. I was missing him as usual and hoped that he would be home before his birthday.

I wanted to give him a birthday party although I felt that might be unlikely since his mother hadn't seen him in so long. I figured she would throw a party for him that I would surely be invited too. At the very least, I was looking forward to being with him to celebrate his birthday since in the previous birthday, he went away. I had dreams of sitting next to him in some fancy restaurant and singing *Happy Birthday* to him while sipping Moet and unwrapping presents.

I would often go back and reread the one letter he sent me quite often holding on to every word. And thought of all the days that I wished that Neville was with me, I don't know how it got to be that I had fully fallen for Neville since he had never even given me a reason to want him, yet alone miss him. There were no special times other than those shared in sexual intimacy.

It was now Thanksgiving, and I was heading to South Dakota to be with my father's family. Ever since my life took a turn for the better financially, I have been going there every year to be with my dad. I loved going there; it reminded me of when I was younger and carefree. This year especially was going to be so much fun because I had money to shop during Black Friday at the outlet mall. Even though I was single and did not really have a man, in everything I did, I thought about Neville. While I was away, I made sure to call his mom and text her to make sure she was doing well during the holiday times. During my shopping spree, I even brought her a Coach wristlet for Christmas. I was so happy that she and I had become so close, and in a way, hoped that this relationship would seal my approval rating to Neville. I genuinely wanted things to be so different between us than the way things were before he went in.

⁓◦⌇◦⁓

Dear Diary:

I can't believe this man has been out for two weeks, and I haven't seen him yet. I am so heartbroken. I have been waiting to see him for more than a year, and he has only called me once. I finally broke down yesterday and told him that I was so disappointed in him. He responded and said that he was basically consumed with his family and that he needed to get that in order first. He explained that he does not have a car right now and that he was busy running around with his kids and others.

His birthday was last week, and I had planned such a lovely date for us but of course he told me that he would be busy at some wedding for his cousin which I did see him posting Facebook pictures. I thought he was going to be celebrating with me, instead I saw him once again having a party with his friends, and he did not invite me. I cried. I cannot understand why he treats me like this. After all he said and all I did, I know it's wrong to expect things in return for the things you do for people, but honestly, I just thought that things would be so different, and I was so sure that Neville had more reasons than ever to want to be with me.

Empress

⦁◦⦁

Christmas break this year was going to be quite different since the girls were going to be spending their vacation with me since their dad chose not to send for them. Despite the many attempts that I made to contact Gary before the break, he refused to respond to me, so I would know whether he was going to taking the children. My lawyer told me he was probably upset about the divorce proceedings since it seemed that I was going to receiving more money than he thought he was going to have to give me. My lawyer had even advised me to not push the issue at this time because he did not want Gary to retaliate in some hateful manner especially against the children. It was interesting that my lawyer had gotten the sense that Gary was childish and capable of such actions. So, having not heard from Gary, I decided that I was going to take the children to Orlando and celebrate Dahlia's birthday and have an early Christmas together for the first time in about four years.

I had kept myself busy since enrolling in a PhD program at Bostic University, and although the time was slowly moving by, it was moving and soon Neville would be home. I had been slowly preparing for his return. And secretively, I had hoped that I would even see him the day he was released.

At this point, I knew that although we had not spoken for four months, there was something about his letter and phone calls; in my mind, there was some glimmer of hope. I knew that beyond a doubt, he loved me and that he appreciated the things that I had done for his family and him while he was away. I knew that he was proud of me and that he would want to show me off as soon as he returned. I imaged the days of loneliness as a memory of the past. I just knew that there would be no more lonely nights, and although, I knew that neither he nor I was ready for totally commitment, I just believed that we were ready to show each other love and affection.

The day had finally come that my phone went off stating that "N. Berger was going to be released today." And although I had to go to work, it was a Teacher Planning Day, I was going to be able to leave work early. I was so excited yet nervous at the same time. It had been so long since I had seen him, and so much had happened in between. I was nervous about seeing him, yet I couldn't wait. I kept checking my phone all day waiting to hear from him. I knew that he would have a lengthy drive back home and that he was supposed to register with the local police department before making any real personal moves.

I just wanted to hear his voice and know that he was going to be coming by to see me. The day seemed to go by so slowly. It was a long wait; it seemed as though more days had been added on to my sentence. I did everything I needed to do for the children that day as usual. I was standing by the sink when suddenly by phone vibrated indicating that I had received a message; it was from Neville.

The message stated that he had just gotten home and that the number he was texting me from was his new cell phone number. He thanked me for everything that I had done and told me that he was going to call me the next day because he was so tired. At that very moment, my heart stopped beating and quickly regained its beat when I reread his message. First, I was glad to see that he was safe back at home, but I was mortified that he could not pick up the phone so that I could hear his voice. I had waited one year to see him, four months, to just to hear his voice and an eternity to be with someone that loved me, but it was slowly unraveling into something that I was not sure I wanted to know what it really was. Even though I was displeased by this display of affection, I accepted it anyway and texted back and said that I was happy that he was home and that I looked forward to hearing from him.

Days passed, he rang my phone three days after he had been out, while I was helping Christiana with her homework. I had not yet assigned a specific ring tone to his contact in my phone so at first, I did not know that it was him calling. When I finally answered the phone, we spoke very casually, and I could hear that he was out. I told him that I was happy to finally hear his voice and that I hoped that we could celebrate his birthday together. He then told me that he had family in town and that they had planned to do various activities with them. I immediately thought about all those times in the past that I had asked him to do various activities with me and he never had the time.

I was so confused and did not really know how to take it all. I knew that being that he had not seen so many of his family members in so long, that he was going to have to see everyone when he came out, but I never expected that I would be the last person in the world that Neville would want to see. It was beyond my imagination, that after all the waiting and sharing, that I would not be with him by now at the least sitting next to him in that restaurant celebrating his birthday.

Days passed and nights pushed through despite the feelings I have, I kept on believing that there would be some magic glue that would put us together. I wanted to believe so much that after being away for so long, that Neville would want to be with me as soon as he could but that was not the case. I often viewed Facebook to see what he was up to since he was barely texting me yet alone calling me nor coming to see me. After two weeks and two days, I saw that he had gone to the Aruba, no less. And I know that it has been a long dream of his to go back to where some of his family was from, but I was flabbergasted that he would leave the country without telling me or seeing me. I am hurt to this day that he would do that to me.

I felt so betrayed, so used, so lonely, so abused, so mistreated, so unloved, so neglected, so untrusted, and so unwanted. It was as if I had been stabbed a million times. My heart cried that night, and my soul became angered. I believed in myself; I needed to believe that I did everything I could do support Neville.

I continued to push myself emotionally, knowing that deep down inside there was all this pain and pressure. Down in my soul was this burning desire to know why things were moving in this direction, but still I let it. I became sick while he was away in Aruba. I guess my body literally broke down after finding out what had transpired. And after going to the doctor, I found out that I had pneumonia. I had decided after two days to contact his mother and let her know that I was sick and on bed rest for the rest of the week.

Shortly thereafter, I had received a text from Neville asking me if I was okay. I knew at that point that his mother had told him that I was sick and not able to go to work. I explained to him that I was sick and hoped to get better soon. Everyday thereafter for the remainder of his trip, he texted me to find out if I was doing better. I would always respond for some reason knowing that this sudden surge of concern was overwhelming my being. It had now been three weeks since he was home, and I had yet to see him. I was slowly feeling more like myself, and I was glad that I was able to once again enjoy the freedom of moving around as I pleased.

I had been cooking in the kitchen and did not realize that I had left my phone upstairs. I was making spaghetti for the kids who loved it; it was one of their favorite dishes. I ran upstairs to see that Neville had texted me two times, indicating that he wanted to come by and see me. Despite the way he treated me and the way he ignored me, I instantly texted him back and told him my address. I began to straighten up the living room furniture and washed the dishes. I began thinking that I was an idiot, but I did not care at that moment to debate the reasons why I should not entertain him at this time.

It had been so long since I had wanted to see him, be next to him, and make love to him that all the other feelings and insecurities went out the door. Instead those feelings were replaced with schoolgirl butterflies and hopes that I forgot existed. When he rang my bell, I ran to the door and opened it like I had just seen Santa Claus on Christmas Day. We hugged so closely, and he kissed me, and instantly all other feelings were irrelevant at that time.

I had so much to say, so much to show him, so much to unfold. Not once did I mention all the wrongs that he had transgressed upon me, not once did I mention the disappointment or dishonor I felt when he abandoned me by going to Aruba or partying with his friends on his birthday. I never mentioned the countless times I expected him to care enough about me to call me to make sure that I was safe. I did not want to spoil the one moment I had with him. I did not want this time to end, so to make the best of it, I only allowed myself to talk about the times I missed him and how I wished that he would just want to have more time together. I only wanted the times that he was with me to last forever. And despite the fact that I knew that I deserved better from a man, I just wanted this man. I just wanted this man to appreciate me, love me, adore me, miss me, touch me, expect of me, desire me, but instead, I had what it was, the moment; and I was determined to make it last.

Dear Diary:

I am just here thinking about last night. I finally got to see Neville. He said that his friend rented a car and that was how he got to see me quite honestly. I did not care how, just that he got here. We finally got to be reunited, and of course, you know that I was elated to see him. He told me that he was proud of me and that he really liked my place. He was surprised to see that I had moved all my belongings because I have a lot of stuff, as he put it. We talked a lot and although we only spent about two hours together, I was grateful.

You already know that everyone thinks that I'm an asshole for allowing this man back into my life, after he treated me the way he did, but I still made love to him, and I enjoyed every moment of it. I cried while we were doing it; the fact that he was with me made me, cry tears of joy. I tried to hold back my true emotions, but they came out anyway. I knew me especially. I cannot hide the way I truly felt about a person.

I love him.

I wished I didn't because I knew that he was not ready for me and that I deserved so much more than he has to offer me right now. Still I cannot explain the levels that I have stooped to attempt to be with Neville. I know that it must end soon, and I am afraid to be alone.

To be honest with you, I am alone now, so I guess I should just accept that fact and try to move on as I have had to do in the past.

Empress

The letters, the calls, the nights and days were all a reflection of my desire to be significant to someone else. I needed to hold fast to my dreams and to focus on my love for my passion, for self- worth, and admiration. I was lonely, and at nights, I stared at the walls and wished that things were different. I prayed for peace and contentment. It was difficult to explain the hurt that each post brought me and how I allowed it to consume me. And with the light that I bear, I could allow someone to pull me so far down that I would be accepting mistreatment and embarrassment.

It was quite a heart fiasco dealing with the ups and downs of our nonexistent relationship. I knew that I was to blame because I allowed myself to become intertwined by lies and empty thoughts and promises that were my foolish translations. I had hoped that one day, Neville could be that man that I needed. I hoped so much that he would save the day and turn into the person I thought he was, instead of me seeing the person he already was. The last day we made love was the last time that I ever saw my friend.

I had no room in my life for imaginary relationships and made-up fairy tales, and despite my letters to Greene County, I gave away a year worth of heartaches for a man that did not want me in the first place.

"For one day, you will find the person who will show you why it never worked out with anyone else, but in the meantime, live your life!"

COMMODITIES AND STOCKS

My children were always my main focus in life. After my first child, Destiney was born by life becoming centered around her activities, her happiness, and just whatever else she may have needed. Eventually that commitment would extend to every one of my children. It was always my position that I would do everything and anything for my children. Thinking back, I couldn't ever remember a time that I did not put my children's well-being before my own. When we first moved to Florida, for example, there were so many days that I would make sure that they had dinner; yet there was not enough for me to eat. I would make sure I could give them lunch money while I worry constantly how I would eat. After a while, I stopped worrying about having fun and just concentrated on raising my children the best way I knew how.

Despite the fact that I was married for fourteen years, I was doing much of what had to be done for the children on my own. In fact, I had gotten so use to putting out the trash, washing the dishes, taking the children to the doctor whenever needed, washing the floor, shoveling snow, cleaning after the animals, or whatever needed to be done to make sure my children were happy and well-taken care of. It appeared while I had been sleeping with someone every night ever since I can remember. I was alone on more than one level ever since day one. I had complained so much about having to always do everything for the children myself while living in New Texas, that I had become accustomed to this way of life, that I had stopped complaining a long time ago and just proceeded to take care of business myself and was quite used to this level of responsibility.

My children were always provoking me to take them back to Mahlia; they had truly enjoyed their visit the last time they were there and were anxious to return. I was also excited with the prospect of their return especially since it is my desire to return to Mahlia one day to live. I really wanted the children to become a little more familiar with the country and how it operated. My wish was for them to travel so much to Mahlia so that people would know who their mother was by looking at them. Despite all those feelings, I knew that since the divorce arrangements, taking the children for an extended stay would be somewhat difficult.

It seemed impossible now because I would now have to work around the times in which I was to have the children, which did not include the summers, the time I traditionally spend the most time there. Mahlia was my get-a-way place, home, somewhere I could hang my hat up and just relax. There was no one there to judge me or to tell me what to do, well at least ever since becoming an adult. The country life was my favorite, which included going to the jungle parties and bar hopping at the local bars. But my ultimate favorite was visiting with family and friends and enjoying the scenes of the beautiful country, and this experience is what I want to share with my daughters.

The first time taking Destiney to Mahlia was when she was about one-year old. She and I had gone there one week prior to my wedding day because my beloved grandmother, on my mother's side, was dying. I had the need to see my grandmother before she left the earth, and believed that if she knew Destiney, she would forever protect her and watch over her. I remembered going to the hospital in Annatto Cove and being by her side. I could still see her sitting up in her hospital bed. I had Destiney next to me and started to comb my grandmother's hair. I kissed her and looked her right in her eyes and told her I loved her. At that very moment, I knew that everything that I ever knew about Mahlia was going to change.

Grandmother was gone and so was grandfather; who would take on the traditions of the family? To this day, no one ever has. I had never had the same experiences in Mahlia as a child when our grandparents, mum, and Mr. B. would flaunt us all over St. Joseph,

Mahlia. Our family had scattered all over the planet, making it extremely difficult to remain as closely knitted as I once remembered it being.

The only thing that was stopping me from going to Mahlia as often as I wanted was money. I was never able to just book a flight at leisure, ever since moving to Florida, and on two different occasions, my sisters had paid for me to travel with them just so we could be together. But to Harmony and Jazmine, it was worth any amount of money so that we could be together in Mahlia; it was our spot; and we traveled there at least once a year together.

Since moving to Florida especially, anytime that we could spend together as sisters was a blessing for all of us. The first time we had traveled to Mahlia was a very interesting trip, and we soon learned to love the travels and fun that was to be had once we arrived there. Our children had the opportunity of being together in Mahlia, twice together, and were just so eager to one day back the trip especially if they could do it together.

My life would forever change the trip during the summer of 2002 when Destiney was diagnosed with a lifelong blood disorder that would forever change the course events for our family. We were traveling to be with our friends and joined them in Top Park for their wedding. It was so beautiful, the flowers, the scenery, even the skeleton of the old hotel that remained on-site; everything just seemed to be so perfect. We had truly enjoyed our time visiting Mahalia including being amongst my family as well; that trip would be the only time my ex-husband Gary would ever meet my family in Mahlia.

We sat at my uncle's table and ate his famous curry chicken and rice and peas; we swam in Blue River; we ate mango on my aunt's veranda and watched the children chase the goats as I had done when I was a girl. It was like a dream come true to return to Mahlia one day with my own family and to make them proud of the parts of this country that their family originated.

My long-time friend Witney, who moved back to Mahlia after graduating college, joined us at the hotel, The Mahlia Grande, for a day of fun with our children while reminiscing of old times in junior high school and experiences we had as mothers. The men, her husband and my husband, were entertaining themselves with stories of their own childhood and memories from Gullie. All seemed to be going well, and the thought of leaving made me very sad which was a feeling that to this day, I get whenever it was time to go away. It seemed to be that the entire family was saddened by the thought of leaving.

On the day before our departure, Destiney had grown lethargic and no sane explanation could be made for her behavior. She became very weak and withdrawn; she was pale and needed assistance just walking. My heart stopped beating and my universe flashed before me not really understanding what was really going on with her behavior or health.

I called my mom and explained to her that Destiney was not feeling herself and that she was seemingly depressed about leaving. I was only hoping for the best, but in the end, it turned out to be the worse.

I never expected motherhood to come with directions and it never did. I did the best that I could do for my children and hoped that they would always know that I went out of my way to create a life for them that was decent and something that they could be proud of.

But at that very moment, none of that mattered because my daughter was struggling, and there was nothing that I could do to help her. I only hoped and prayed that I could return to New Texas in time for her to see her doctor and receive medication for whatever she may have picked up during the trip. The only diagnosis I could possible image at the time was that she had ingested something that had made her sick, little did I know.

We finally made it to LJP airport, and Destiney could barely walk, so we had to seek the help of the airport personnel and secure a wheelchair for her. While waiting for Gary to get the taxi, I could see her panting and gasping for breath, to say that was the scariest sight that I had ever seen was an understatement. To see my baby in a wheelchair and helpless to assist her was truly any mother's worse nightmare. We quickly got everyone situated in the taxi and pro-ceeded to ask the driver if he could stop at the local pharmacy as we approached our home. We purchased some Tylenol at the pharmacy and headed straight home.

Upon entering the house, I immediately called the doctor and left a message with the emergency pager and waited patiently for the doctor to return my call. Since the doctor usually called me back quickly, I laid down next to Destiney and hoped that the Tylenol would bring down her fever and make her feel better.

I soon jumped up when I realized the doctor had not called back, and I had fallen asleep exhausted from all the day's events and then looked at Destiney. I could see that she was continually struggling to breathe, and at that moment, I made the decision to take her to the emergency room. Gary made the decision to stay home with Vanessa as it was late, and we did not want to take Vanessa out the house at such a late hour. Even more, we did not know what was going to be in store for us.

Upon arriving at the emergency room, I was surprised to see the number of patients that were waiting since it was so early in the morning. After signing Destiney in, we waited for about ten minutes before being seen by the doctor. The first thing I remembered doing was crying. I had never been in an emergency room for my children, and I was alone; this was to be the first of many days that I would spend alone with Destiney at the hospital. When the nurse called her name, I literally had to pick Destiney up to take her to the intake room. Seeing Destiney's condition, the nurse told me to just bring her straight to the bed. The nurse took her vitals, drew blood, and it was then determined by the ER doctors that she was going to ICU.

To this day, I swore it all took place in a matter of five seconds, the night my life turned all around.

I quickly called Gary and informed him that Destiney was very sick and that there was no diagnosis yet but that she was requiring blood transfusions and needed to be given oxygen due to loss of blood and oxygen. All I kept thinking to myself was, *did she pick up a virus? Was she going to be alright? What was happening to my child at that very moment, To see the tubes, the blood, the needles and to know that I could not take her place and that she would need me to be strong enough to help her fight whatever was going on in her body?*

The days turned to nights, and she was not getting better. I stayed with her and at times took breaks with Gary, so I could go home and shower. He would bring us food, and most days, sat in the same place. I was smoking cigarettes at the time to escape whenever I could, to go downstairs, to run away from the stress that I was feeling watching my daughter suffer. Doctors could not offer us with any solution, just the promise of more testing until a diagnosis could be made.

A few days had passed, and soon, I had forgotten what day of the week it was. Many medical tests were conducted on my daughter including a spinal tap that I literally broke down and just cried myself to sleep when it was time for the doctor to perform it. Destiney was subjected to countless blood tests, x-rays, sonograms, specialty doctor visits, and so many other rather exhausting exams for the doctors to determine that she had some type of blood disorder. This blood disorder had basically taken over her blood, and it had started to break itself away. To hear of such news brought sadness to my life and pain to my heart; it brought questions to my mind and tests to my life; it brought strength I never knew I had and courage I wish I never had to show, but what it mostly brought, was true love and hope, that all the best would be for my children no matter what was currently happening in our lives.

Dear Diary:

Today was the first time in a long time that I went to get my nails done. Destiney has finally got out of the hospital, and I just couldn't wait to be able to be myself again. I had to take her to the doctor now just about every week until she becomes more stable, to have her blood drawn so that the doctors can continue to monitor her to see if she will need more blood transfusions. While in the hospital, she had blood given to her four separate times to just get her levels back to where they needed to be. The doctors predicted that she will need to get transfusions if her blood continued to go down, in the meantime, they have placed her on steroids, and it had caused her to gain a lot of weight. It was very stressful here at home too just trying to get things back in order.

I have done so much laundry recently, and my back is killing me; the laundry sat here piled up while I was in the hospital with Destiney. I was expecting to return back to work next week, and honestly, I am just not ready. I hope that Destiney will be alright when returning to school; she's so fragile. I worry constantly about her, and recently, it has just taken over all my thoughts. Meanwhile, while Destiney was in the hospital, Gary had a DNA test done on Stephanie, and it was determined that Stephanie was not his child. With everything going on, it's just been another added pressure because this news was something I've always hoped for. That girl's mother has ruined so many moments of my married life, and it turned out that she is not even Gary's child. To say that I am relieved is truly an understatement, and I hope that he will be able to deal with it since so far, he has not really been talking about what has just been discovered; perhaps he was too preoccupied with thoughts of what was going on with Destiney.

A lot had happened. I even lost some weight; it looked a little scary because I haven't been this thin in a while, but I am hoping that I will soon be able to gain the weight back. In any case, I am going to lay on the couch and watch some television until I fall asleep, and as usual, when

Gary is ready to go upstairs, he will wake me up, and we will go to bed. Until next time.

Empress

❧

The girls were going to be having their first recital soon, and I was so excited to be able to dress them up in makeup and fancy buns like my mom had done for me. I had of course volunteered to be a backstage mother and help with the shenanigans that takes place with two hundred little girls waiting behind closed curtains just to perform. I had totally forgot to buy flowers before arriving to the show, so as soon as the show was over, I quickly ran over to the table where the vendors were all set up, waiting for proud parents such as myself, who just did not find the time to buy gifts prior to arriving at the high school where the show took place.

I bought flowers and balloons for both girls and wobbled myself over to where the kids were exiting. My mother was by my side and waited with me while Gary went to retrieve the girls from the side exit door. Even though I was pregnant, I tried really hard not to be bothered by the heat and crowd. I was so happy that I was able to volunteer with the other dance moms and had suggested that the family go out to eat afterward at our favorite local diner, The Upscaled Diner.

I decided that I wanted to have another baby and hoped so bad that it was a boy. My mother had lost her son, my brother; he was stillborn, and the thought of the repeated cycle scared me half to death. I prayed day and night for a boy and decided that I was not going to find out what gender the baby was until it had arrived. I had hopes also of using my new born baby's cord blood to one day save her sister's life through either research or donation. However, it turned out that I would not be able to make use of that initial idea.

I prayed, day and night, that God would see fit to allow me to have a son. I could always hear the words of Marcia saying that I was not a real woman because I never had any boys; she just hated me.

Those same words haunted me to this day as I never did have any sons.

I thought about it with each passing month and had decided that I was not going to find out the gender of the baby until it was born. That mystery was one that I could not wait to solve and was looking forward to my last sonogram to make sure that the baby was developing healthy.

I arrived at the appointment for the sonogram, about thirty minutes early and was so eager to be in my final stages of pregnancy. I was escorted into the room where the sonogram was going to be performed and the nurse gave garments to change into so that the technician could perform her tests. As the technician began to scan the baby, I could feel the baby jump and kick inside of me. It was a feeling that was incomparable to no other in this world. The thought of adding another human being to my family was something that brought me extreme joy and admiration. I felt that this baby was going to somehow be the salvation to all of Destiney's medical problems and possibly bring Gary and I closer to together, at least I hoped.

After the technician had performed all her standard tests, she asked me if I wanted to know the sex of the baby. In my heart, I knew that I had made a promise to myself that I would not find out and that I would be happy as long as the baby was healthy, but I soon fell victim to curiosity. With a solemn and stern face, I replied, "Yes, I do want to know."

And with that she said, "Congratulations, Ms. Braxton; you are having a girl."

At that very moment, my heart dropped, and I lost my thoughts.

I became warm and flustered and the need for water was real.

I proceeded to gather my thoughts and thank the technician for her assistance as she instructed me that I could get dressed. As I began to put my clothes back on, I could feel the tears run down my face, and I could hear my baby say, "Mommy, I love you." And at that moment, I realized that this baby would be very special in my life, that her presence would fill a very big void in our lives and that she would somehow be the one to capture the hearts of so many that she meets.

When she was born, we named her Christina and to this day, she was the daughter that mostly resembled me. She is my hero, my inspiration; she has been there for me as a daughter, and I love her dearly. It appeared, from the day Christina was born; our lives would be forever different, and learning to be a family from this day forward would be something that we would need to do if we were to survive.

$$\sim\!\!\odot\!\!\sim$$

Dear Diary:

Today I noticed that Christina had some bruising on her legs and arms. I also noticed that her fingernails were getting yellow. From past experiences with Destiney, I realized that something must be going on with her. I called Dr. Vi right away, and she told me to bring her into the office as soon as I got from work. When I arrived at the doctor's office, Chrissy went in for blood work. I cried as I watched my eighteen-month-old baby being poked and prodded by the doctors and simultaneously was reliving the events that have taken place with Destiney. It was so hard to experience it as a mother especially because she was so tiny. Her little face and hands were just reaching out for me; it was simply heartbreaking.

After leaving the doctor's office, Pamela, Dr. Vi's secretary, called me back to tell me that Chrissy's blood counts were low and that she was going to need a transfusion. I cannot begin to tell you how I'm feeling right now. I will be taking off from work tomorrow to bring her into the hospital. The hospital made me sick just the sight of it; it smelled like alcohol, and it made me nauseate. The amount of time that I have been spending at the hospital with Destiney alone made my head spin. I lost five pounds in the last month, and I didn't see it getting any easier. So, the transfusion was scheduled to take place at 9:00 am, so I better get some rest for I know. I will need the energy to deal with the emotional war that will about to take place in my heart.

I was just going to wash the dishes and check on the kids and sleep on the couch until it's time to go upstairs as usual. Hope we will get some good news soon and not have to continue with blood transfusions; they really scare me, and I could only imagine how it makes the girls feel.

Empress

✧◦◦◦✧

Days and nights of praying and hoping that God would see fit to heal my children of this mystery that had taken over them, my Destiney and Christina had to endure sonograms, cat scans, MRI, spinal taps, weekly blood work, blood transfusions, tears, pain, agony, missing friends, missing family, missing life, and all I could do for them was pray. It was one of the most heart-wrenching experiences I have ever endured. To watch your children struggle for life, to see the pain in their eyes, to want to exchange places but couldn't, to want to tell them that it would all be okay but knowing that it might not was—is the scariest thing that as a mother, I have ever endured—endure.

This was a heartache that no mother should have to endure. I would not wish the pain and agony that my family had experienced on my worst enemy. And people always say it could be worse, and maybe they are correct, but my God, PLEASE spare my children, all of them, from any more pain.

Vanessa never complained. She always smiled, always did well in school, never gave us any worries; perhaps she knew we have enough worries.

We lived with uncertainty everyday not knowing if the children will continue to exhibit more symptoms. They had been seen by countless doctors, specialists, the Institute of Health, and others that proclaim to know about ways that they can treat their illness. But I am going just keep believing in my God for complete healing and pray that one day I will be able to come back with the testimony that my children are completely healed from their ailments.

Now when I looked into my daughter Dahlia's eyes, what I saw was promise. I conceived her knowing that my husband and I would probably not stay together, but once again, I had hopes that a baby could somehow change the course of events that were already underway. I planned to have one last baby before I would have my tubes tied making it official that the baby-making days would be over for me.

Before I could even leave the hospital, I had an appointment to come back the following week to have my tubes tied. I figured that if I would be starting a new life soon, I would not want the complication of pregnancy, and I was never a major fan of having more than one baby dad anyway. I was known in the family as "fertile myrtle" since it seemed like I was getting pregnant like every three years, and that was because most people did not know that all my children were planned.

While at the time, it seemed like the best idea; later I did question whether I had made the best decision regarding tying my tubes at that time. In the end, I did think it was the best thing for me or else I might have at least had another baby by now, and the worse part, it would have been with a man that never loved me, *just had love for me*, his exact words.

Dahlia Zynia was my last commodity created by the union that was once called my marriage. She was simply perfect, born with grey eyes, shiny silky black hair, pale skin, and the cutest dimples ever, and while they all shared similar traits at birth, Dahlia was the only one born with grey eyes. She was quiet as a baby, never really cried much or made a fuss. While growing up, she took her place in the household of five ladies, and while she was the baby sister, she never let any one of them bully her into anything. Head strong and independent from birth and seemingly always just in the know and hip to what was taking place around her, Dahlia was my last stock in procreation, and she was making me so proud every day.

⁓◉⌒

Dear Diary:

Today I finally sat down and told Gary that I am leaving him; he didn't believe me. He kept asking me where I was going, and to tell you the truth right now, I really didn't know. I was researching Tola because Gary always thought that was a nice area to relocate to. Right now, I am focusing on Florida, but I needed to know where I could go and make money; it did not seem that, that state pays like NYT does and that securing an administrative position was going to be difficult there. Right now, I have a lot to think about. Dahlia was only one, and I was scared to be alone. I haven't been alone since I was twenty-one years old, and now I have four children. Gary kept telling me that I will never make it without him. He also reminded me that I was a single mom, and no one wants someone with four kids.

I was so afraid that I would end up as an old lonely woman after my kids grow up. I'll end up dying alone, but God, I just couldn't take living here one more day. I felt so torn; what am I doing tearing my family apart? I should just live the rest of my days miserable but married, my children with their father. Maybe one day, I could learn to love him the way I used to and regain the passion. But how long will that take? And will it ever happen that way, or will I be just wishing my life away? When I looked into the children eyes, I saw hope. I was hoping that the love that they give me will be enough to sustain me when I am lonely. I knew that they will understand, and one day, they will be able to forgive me for taking them away from their father, but there was no way I was ever going to leave my children behind. One day, I asked Destiney and Vanessa if they wanted to move to Florida with me, and they immediately replied, "Mom, we want to go with you."

I was so scared. I was so afraid and lost. I had no direction except that of the Lord, and I prayed that would be enough to get me through this. Until later.

Empress

I didn't have many personal possessions in this world. I had never learned how to increase my wealth or how to save for the future. I planned my life month by month for so long that I forgot to look at the big picture. My children were my stocks, my commodities; they were my investments. Everything I ever was or ever hoped to be, I poured into them and for these reasons, I know that my greatest return in life shall come from them.

PRIVATE MATTERS

I was seventeen years old when I graduated from high school, and ever since then, I knew that I was going to make something out of my life. Despite the setbacks and obstacles that I had seen in life, I was determined that by no way was that going to shape my future. I was always very strong-minded and conditioned to believe that it was my destiny to be a mark in society, no matter how small. And despite that fact that I was an accomplished educator, there was a need and yearning to achieve more. For that reason, I wanted to pursue every dream I ever had. The best feeling in life was for me to accomplish some goal that I had set for myself.

I sat down for the first time yesterday to read over some papers that I was sorting out to throw away. It hadn't dawn on me that it had been so long since I had cleaned out my file cabinet, and clearly, there were things that needed to go. It was a painstaking task for me since every single piece of paper seemed so important. In many ways, I was a lot like my father; he never could throw anything away. I shifted through all the medical records and convinced myself that I only needed to save those that I had obtained within the last month. There were so many documents that I had saved since filing the divorce, thinking that each one was more important than the other. The draws that contained these papers were literally flowing over, so I was more determined than ever to make sense out of this mounting mess.

The children were gone for the summer as had been the custom since separating from their father, and I had become immune to the silence and extra time that came when four children all left the house at the same time. While the summer months brought an opportunity to regroup and refresh my mind, it always was a quiet time that brought much reflection and loneliness. In my heart, it was a glimpse of what my life would be like once the children had grown up and left me. I spent many nights wondering if there would ever be some-one with whom I could share my life with, my secrets with, my life, my body. For many reasons, I constantly thought about my future and what it might entail for me. I had always envisioned my life as so much more than just being a schoolteacher and mother. I wanted so much to continue to strive for those things that I desired to have. And despite all the things that I had accomplished in many ways, I was scared to be alone in my own bed at nights. I prayed for many days to be comforted in some way by the words or hugs or touches of a man that really loved me.

I knew and believed that loneliness was not going to be a part of my forever, so for the time being, I focused on myself and goals.

There were many nights that paperwork filing would continue as well as the endless shots of rum I took just to ease the pains of the empty house. Christina would call me every day just to hear my voice even if I only had time for a quick hello and goodbye. One night, I laid back on the couch just turning to reflect on the many experiences I had in life. Tears instantly rolled down my face as I could feel my emotions began to choke me, and I fell into a trance that paralyzed me. I had been in this space before, and I knew what it felt like, so it scared me to think that views of my past were about to flash before my eyes. Thoughts danced around me of failures and what ifs. Times of joy followed by times of rage took over my mind while I stared heavily at the degrees that hung on the wall. I could not help but to think about all the time and effort I put into attaining these pieces of paper.

The ultimate sacrifice that I would make in life was to invest in my education and personal growth. And yet, all I could think about was the empty feeling I had inside. Knowing that for so long, I had given my all to my children and hoped that I had not forgotten to ensure my own happiness. As I sat on the couch, I saw the faces of those that betrayed me and those that said that I could never amount to anything. I could hear their words repeatedly saying things like,

"You're nothing, you're not even a real woman, you are all used up and no one will ever want you." In many ways, I could vividly hear each one as if they were loud and clearly speaking right next to me. I felt a sense of helplessness as I had realized that the sands of time were quickly accumulating and that before I knew it, I would be running low on time. I felt as though time was against me and that nothing that I could do would ever bring back those experiences that had aged me.

My education was the only thing that I truly had that no one could take away from me was what I kept thinking inside. While I continued to strive to be a better person socially, there was a real desire in me to reach a level that could possibly help me to evacuate the current social class that I currently occupied. I had finally decided that it was time to pursue the dreams and goals that I had always had, the dreams of being free and alone and trying to decide what was the next steps. As I listened to my heart, I could hear it say that it was lonely and that it needed to find someone to share my life with. I was tired of hearing that I was a good friend but not a person that he wanted to be with. I had decided that I needed to focus more on my destiny rather than focusing on a relationship with my mystery man that I might not ever meet.

◦◦◦

Dear Diary:

    I woke up again at 3:00 am, and I just couldn't figure out why I kept getting up so early. People told me that when you have a lot on your mind, it's hard to sleep soundly through the night; well that might have some truth to it. I had been thinking about everything going on with my life, and it made me wonder about the children and what would happen to them if something were to happen to me. I never had life insurance so one of the things I decided to do was to get some life insurance and invest in some stocks or something so that if I die, my kids would have something to help them get started in life. I made an appointment with a personal financial advisor on Tuesday afternoon. I knew that I was not going to be here forever, so I knew that I needed to think about what would happen to the girls once I leave this Earth.

It scared me to think that they might have to grow up without me and that I would not live long enough to see them grow up or to see my grandchildren. I talked to the kids the other day about growing up and what they want to do in the future. I was so excited to see if they will do the things that they talked about now. I knew that I pretty much wanted to be a teacher since I went to college, and I could not ever remember wanting to do anything else.

I prayed many days that I would get the chance to grow old with someone that I love. I sometimes regret the fact that I became a teacher because I wished that I had a job that made more money. I made sure to discuss that with the children that making a good amount of money was important when they were looking to choose an occupation in the future. The children were always my biggest concern. And ensuring that they were prepared for the future was ultimately my biggest concern.

I was going to try to go back to sleep after I went and made a cup of tea; hopefully I will be able to go back to sleep shortly. Talk to you soon.

Empress

It was going to be a fun day because I was going to surprise the children and tell them that I had bought tickets to Universal Studies in Orlando. I had wanted to take them somewhere, vacationing so badly; at that same time, I decided that it was going to be just me and the girls. It was time that we had a family trip, and ever since getting child support, I knew that I was going to be able to take them this year. I had also thought ahead about taking them somewhere during the break in March and inviting my mother to go with us. This was going to be a wonderful time to be with the children.

It seemed to me at that time that although I was still getting my head out of the water; things were looking up and things were going to be alright for the children and me. I knew that gone were the days of an empty fridge and not knowing if we could afford to enjoy our life. The children and I had suffered long enough, and I was ready to spoil them rotten to make up for all the times that I could not afford to buy them the things that needed and deserved. We were going to the movies, out to eat, shopping, making plans, and just not being stressed out over being able to pay the bills. Sometimes I wondered why I ever had to be stressed out the way I was trying to support the children, but I was happy that things had changed, so I decided that this day forward, I was not going to be reminded about the past and instead that I was going to live in the present.

My mother always told me that silver and gold would fade away, but a good education would never decay; growing up, I never really understood what that meant, but as I grew up, I truly appreciated my education. It was a motto that I grew up believing in, and it showed in the pride I took in the education that I had obtained. Thinking back, it was the one thing that I could depend on; it supported my children when I had almost nothing; it moved me up the ranks in NYT rather quickly, and it was currently going to be the bridge that would connect my past and my future.

I could never stop moving forward to seek those things that I had always wanted. It was another vehicle that would lead to bigger and greater things.

At night, I could still hear Gary's words saying, "You'll never be anything without me; no one would ever want you," and I was determined that, that was not going to be destiny.

I realized that I was the only one that could control how the tables were going to turn. I was that one person who could make things better for myself and my family. And the need to make it happen was real. It was the silent prayer that I said every night, so God would have mercy on my family, and I show us favor. I was up late at night worrying if I would ever find someone that was going to be real with me, and it was scary to think of my life alone once the children left.

Ever since Destiney had decided to leave my house at the age of seventeen to go live with her father, I started to think about life without the children and what I would be doing with my time in the future. I had decided that I was going to go live in Mahlia once the children had grown older, and that was going to be my mission and never again was I going to let someone's words keep me from believing that I could achieve anything that I had set my mind to do.

∽⊙∾

Dear Diary:

Today I am forty years old, and I am so blessed to see this day. I had invited a lot of my friends and family to Florida to celebrate with me. My parents, aunt Levern, uncle Thomas, Monique, Jazmine, Peter Gaye, Olivio, Amoretta, Ray, and many others from work and my hang-out partners are going to join me at this club that I rented out to have my party. We will be cooking so much food, and Jazmine would not let me do any of the cooking because I have a cold. It has been a lot of work organizing everything, but I am excited.

I just received a call from Neville saying that he's not going to be able to make it which makes me very sad. He said that he really wanted to be there but for some reason, I had doubts that he did everything he could to be able to be there. I didn't know why I kept expecting different results with him. In any case, I planned to drink, smoke, eat and enjoy the company of those people that are going to be there. I will have to try to ignore the fact that Neville has never attended any of the life events that I have had and that I have invited him to attend.

I had asked Daryl to take pictures of the event seeing that he was a professional, but I was still quite disappointed with the way everything turned out with him. After all, he misled me as to who he was since we had met on a dating website, and that really changed the nature of our relationship and trust. I never wanted to believe that finding someone had to be this difficult, but it seemed that while everyone was so successful with their love lives, mine was going nowhere. After the party, I could never find myself to talk with Daryl again because of the betrayal that I felt from him. I was never again able to trust another word that came out of his mouth.

My party is beginning to get started, and I am nowhere ready and of course, instead of getting ready, I'm here writing in my journal; it helps with the stress. I was trying the best I can to remain positive although I felt like shit, and all I want to do was to be with someone special on my birthday. Let me go now and get myself together before another person comes in my room to ask me if I am ready; mind you it is 1:00 am. In a way, maybe I am stalling because I know that there will be no one there that I can cut my cake with or kiss after the first dance. I am going to write to you later and let you know how everything went as soon as I sober up the next day.

Until later,
Empress

᭣᭣᭣

I understood why they said blood is thicker than water; my family came out for my birthday and really helped me to celebrate in style. I was so happy that my sisters were there except the eldest one who has never been close because of her constant jealousy of my father, who was not her father. She told my dad that she was not coming to my birthday party because I did not call her and personally invited her to the attend the party.

Like I told my dad, I would never understand why she was so jealous. I explained to my dad that it would be like calling everyone who got invited to my wedding; furthermore, I felt she was lucky I had invited her.

In the end, I understood the only thing that woman ever wanted was to rob my sisters and I of everything my father owned. She never bet on the fact that the love that my sisters and I have for each other was greater than any amount of dollars that she stole from us. That the love the family shares can easily dry up and never flow again.

It was the best birthday ever except one thing. I had no one there as my partner, no one to cut my cake with or kiss or go home with and cuddle up after the night had ended. I was, once again, by myself.

I heard the rain falling so hard. It scared me at first because it was coming so quickly. I had forgotten to take the grill inside so the last of the coals were getting wet. The smelter fire smelled like Mahlia and somehow, I could see breadfruit roasting in the fire. As I came inside, the guests were sitting there waiting for me to just sit down and enjoy the party. Sitting down was just not something that I was used to doing. I often found that when I had company. I was the busiest because I wanted to make sure that everyone was comfortable and enjoying themselves.

Jazmine has just finished frying a batch of her famous empanadas, and everyone talked about how good they tasted. All I could think about was how happy I was that my family was here to celebrate these occasions with me, including Vanessa's graduation from High School, and Destiney was twenty-one also.

These moments were especially difficult after the death of our king, and in many ways, my sisters and I were always going to grieve the loss of our father. Being together during this time was especially significant and even better now that the house was filled with drunk guests that were all here to celebrate the festivities. We ate, talked, and swam in the pool. The party had a good vibe going until Neville walked in. Those that knew of Neville were surprised to see him as I had been hiding the fact that I had still been sleeping with him after all the disappointments he had brought. I stopped talking about him with my friends for fear that they would jeer me and talk about how dumb I was once I walked away.

I could not admit to them that secretly I always hoped that he would grow up and change his ways, stop playing with my emotions, that somehow he would just ignore me and leave me alone since he was not interested in being in a committed relationship with me. I could not tell my family and friends that I was still dealing with his foolishness. And when he walked in the party and kissed me on the lips in front of everyone, all those other worries once again left my thoughts.

The party was halted when three police cars showed up in front of my home; apparently one of my new neighbors had called them complaining of the noise since I had hired a DJ; perhaps they were not used to the level we were pumping. I proceeded to go to speak with the police and inform them that we were going to turn down the music. As I returned to the backyard where most of the adults gathered, I noticed that Neville had gotten up from where he was sitting. I asked him if everything was okay and he began making his way to the front of the house. He told me that he wanted to move his car because he was parked on the neighbor's front lawn. I informed him that I would be washing the dishes and waiting for him inside.

Ten minutes passed by and I noticed that Neville had not returned yet. I began calling his phone, no answer. I called again,

again no answer. On the third try he finally picked up. I asked him where he had gone and if everything was alright. He said he was on his way home.

He never even said goodbye.

He never gave me a kiss good night.

That summer, I saw him for a total of ten minutes. It was the sixth year of me knowing Neville and many times I walked away physically but obviously mentally I was still tied.

Imagine that, I thought, *another summer of tears and sorrow, another summer of wishing and hoping and wanting to have something that is all my own.* I had once again fallen for the empty conversations, hopeful texts, the quick visits and meaningless intimate affairs. In many ways, I wanted so badly to forget Neville, but every time I tried, he came up again.

Dear Diary:

The children are all home this summer. Christina had been receiving chemo for her lung disorder and planning it where her father lives was not working out. As a result, I asked her father if they could spend the summer with me this year, and of course without hesitation, they were here. It had been a busy summer, not one that I am used to. I usually have quiet and so much free time. But this year, I have had so many out-of-town guests and the girls, so things have been very busy around here. Peter Gaye even came down to spend time with me and see the new house which was a fun time truly. We hung out, went shopping and talked for hours like college kids, late nights in a college dorm.

I took the kids to the food truck explosion, and sometimes, we would go out for Narvella

Ice cream which was one of their favorites even from back in New Texas. We went school-supply shopping and eventually bought clothes and shoes to prepare for the rapidly approaching new school year.

Sometimes I really get tired of thinking about going back to middle school for another year but that was what it is looking like for me again. Perhaps I needed a fire put under my ass.

We will talk soon.

Empress

⚬⊙⚬

The dog was barking, but I did not care. I continued to find pleasure in what I was doing. It bothered me sometimes that I was subjected to battery-operated pleasure, but it was at sometimes the highlight of my entire week.

I kept the motions, up and down hoping that I could find the spot that created a temporary smile. I wanted to lose myself with myself in the hopes that I could forget that it had been so long since I had been intimate, with a man.

I had many suitors that wanted to exchange position with my toys, but I had built a wall that excluded all those who were not Neville.

Neville had been the man of pleasure for the last four years, and it really scared me to think of starting over in such uncertain times. And while I had come to the obvious conclusion that Neville was receiving female companionship from others since it had not been with me for so long, I still felt that being with one man was some-how better than being with others. I knew damn well that was not the case; it's possible other lovers were my lovers since we were not actually using condoms.

I could NEVER tell anyone that I was having sex with Neville without condoms; they would be so disappointed in me. Still I continued this practice, thinking that somehow this would make us closer and that was probably why I allowed it despite knowing better. He had been the only one that I allowed since leaving my husband to be with him and that we were not using condoms. I was slowly turning into bigger a fool.

✺

Dear Diary:

Once again, I made up all kinds of excuses for this man; he made me feel so incomplete. I once again waited on him after cooking, and he never even showed up or called to say that he was not stopping by at all; who does something like this to someone they love? Why is this happening to me? How could someone you love treat you so bad?

I guess I was just frustrated because I didn't want to accept the truth. The fact was a man can never really love two women at the same time because one of them wasn't going to be loved as much as the other and many times not even shown any love at all.

I hope that one day, I could build up the strength to forget about the lies, promises, and that one letter (the only time I ever saw his handwriting), so that I could fall in love again with someone who really loves me.

As I sit here and think about my many experiences, I had reached to this conclusion, dance in the rain, run in the forest, walk in the light for only I can do what I need to do for me.

Empress

ABOUT THE AUTHOR

Zylia N. Knowlin is the mother of four girls. She currently resides in South Florida. She has spent the last twenty-two years educating middle-school students on topics concerning American and World History and Geography. Over the years, she has maintained her daily journals and wanted to share some of life experiences with young people across the world.

After completing her PhD program (2020), she has plans on writing curriculum and initiating programs that prevent domestic violence and child violations in Jamaica, West Indies. Proceeds from this publication will be used in part to fund the JASWA (Jamaican American Social and Welfare Alliances) Project she is currently building.

CPSIA information can be obtained
at www.ICGtesting.com
Printed in the USA
LVHW050009071020
668069LV00006B/570